SNOWBOUND
The Record of a Theatrical Touring Party

THE DESERT ISLAND DRACULA LIBRARY

promotes the study of Dracula, vampirism, and the works of Bram Stoker

SNOWBOUND: THE RECORD OF A THEATRICAL TOURING PARTY
Bram Stoker - Annotated by Bruce Wightman 1-874287-29-5

THE PRIMROSE PATH
Bram Stoker – Introduced by Richard Dalby 1-874287-21-X

DRACULA: SENSE & NONSENSE
Elizabeth Miller 1-874287-24-4

DRACULA: THE SHADE AND THE SHADOW
Edited by Elizabeth Miller 1-874287-10-4

DRACULA UNEARTHED
Annotated by Clive Leatherdale 1-874287-12-0

DRACULA: THE NOVEL AND THE LEGEND – A STUDY OF BRAM STOKER'S GOTHIC MASTERPIECE
Clive Leatherdale 1-874287-04-X

THE ORIGINS OF DRACULA – THE BACKGROUND TO BRAM STOKER'S GOTHIC MASTERPIECE
Clive Leatherdale 1-874287-07-4

TREATISE ON VAMPIRES AND REVENANTS – THE PHANTOM WORLD
Dissertation on those Persons who Return to Earth Bodily, the Excommunicated, the Oupires or Vampires, Vroucolacas, &c
Dom Augustine Calmet 1-874287-06-6

THE JEWEL OF SEVEN STARS
Bram Stoker – Annotated by Clive Leatherdale 1-874287-08-2

THE LADY OF THE SHROUD
Bram Stoker – Annotated by William Hughes 1-874287-22-8

THE SHOULDER OF SHASTA
Bram Stoker – Annotated by Alan Johnson 1-874287-30-9

A GLIMPSE OF AMERICA: AND OTHER LECTURES, INTERVIEWS & FEATURES
Introduced by Richard Dalby 1-874287-35-X

SNOWBOUND

THE RECORD OF A THEATRICAL TOURING PARTY

by

BRAM STOKER

ANNOTATED AND EDITED BY
BRUCE WIGHTMAN

Series Editor: Clive Leatherdale

Desert Island Books Limited

First Published in United Kingdom in 1908
This annotated edition published in 2000

DESERT ISLAND BOOKS LIMITED
89 Park Street, Westcliff-on-Sea, Essex SS0 7PD
United Kingdom
www.desertislandbooks.com

British Library Cataloguing-in-Publication Data
A catalogue record for this book is available from
the British Library

ISBN 1-874287-29-5

Printed in Great Britain
by
Biddles Ltd, Guildford

Contents

Preface

The Truth – or rather Accuracy – of these Stories may be accepted or not as the Reader pleases. They are given as Fiction.

BRAM STOKER

The cast of *Snowbound* in order of appearance (this list was not presented in the 1908 edition):

Acting (Business) Manager (MC)	Mr Wragge
Actor Manager	Mr Benville Nonplusser
Leading Lady	Miss Venables
Wardrobe Mistress Sewing Woman ('Ma')	Miss Wrigglesworth
First Low Comedian ('Gags')	Mr Parmentire
Prompter	Mr Gallimant
Second Low Comedian	Mr Hupple
Young Gentleman	Mr Horatio ('Bloze') Sparbrook
Second Heavies	Mr Hemans
Singing Chambermaid	
Tragedian ('Bones')	Mr Wellesley Dovercourt
Super-Master	Mr Murphy
Advance Agent	Mr Montague Alphage
Master Machinist	Mr Hempitch
Scene Painter	Mr Turner Smith

Other members of the touring company mentioned but not invited to tell a tale: Call Boy (Brooke); Property Master (Mr Ruggles); Baggage Master; Heavy Father; Leading Juvenile (Dandy); First Old Woman; Young Man; Second Old Woman; Musical Director; Stage Manager.

Bibliographical Note

SNOWBOUND is among the rarest and least seen of all Bram Stoker's literary oeuvre. Its scarcity is due mainly to the fact that the first (and only) previous edition was issued as an ephemeral delicate paperback – over ninety years ago – never designed to last for more than a few years at most. Nearly all copies would have been discarded quickly, and possibly only a small fraction might have entered public libraries stoutly rebound in cloth.

In over thirty years of collecting Stoker's first editions, I have seen only three rebound ex-library copies, but none in the original pristine paperback wrappers. The Bodleian Library copy is rebound, retaining the pictorial front cover showing the snowbound train (in the winter Scottish wilderness) somewhere between the Grampians and the North Sea.

The 256-page paperback was published in December 1908, possibly aimed for the Christmas market, in 'Collier's Shilling Library'. For almost the entire Edwardian decade, from 1902 to 1909, Stoker's books were published by William Heinemann. Though, chronologically, *Snowbound* lies midway between *Lady Athlyne* (June 1908) and *The Lady of the Shroud* (July 1909), it was published instead by the small London company of Collier & Co (2 Tudor Street, EC).

My Story, the autobiography of Hall Caine, was published in the autumn of 1908 by Collier in conjunction with Heinemann (with both names appearing on the title page), so the two companies might have been closely linked at this time. Stoker and Caine – who was then among Britain's most popular living novelists – had been very close friends for some twenty years.

After Sir Henry Irving's death in 1905, Stoker concentrated not only on his own literary career but also worked as Caine's literary agent. Throughout the summer of 1908 he had been occupied in editing Caine's over-long autobiography, eventually cutting out 15,400 words with the author's approval. Caine's elder son, Ralph, had joined Collier & Co in 1907 and assisted in the production of *My Story*, alongside Stoker and Collier's manager, Adam Cranston.

Assuming that *Snowbound* had been rejected by Heinemann, it seems likely that this volume saw print thanks to the joint advisory efforts of Hall Caine (in gratitude for Stoker's help earlier that year) and his son Ralph.

The name of this small London publisher suggests a connection with the popular American magazine, 'Collier's' – owned and run by Peter Fenelon Collier (1849-1909) – but this is not proven. The verso of the title page gives two copyright dates of '1899' and '1908'. These seem to imply that the stories in *Snowbound* may have been serialised in a magazine during 1899, but again there is no evidence for this.

Several researchers have combed through 'Collier's Magazine' from the mid-1890s up to 1909 without finding a single contribution by Stoker, and no trace of any of the *Snowbound* stories in any magazine, American or British. The '1899' date remains a bibliographical mystery.

The stories themselves provide a fascinating insight into theatrical touring life at the turn of the century; and reflect the group storytelling flair so beloved of the innumerable Christmas Numbers created by Dickens, Collins, Mrs Gaskell and their contemporaries.

Richard Dalby

Introduction

It is extraordinary that to the public at large Bram Stoker remains a 'one book author'. Shout the name *Dracula* and the world responds; shout the name of his author and until recently there was virtually no reaction at all. For that reason alone, Desert Island Books are to be congratulated for bringing his other works to wider attention.

My delight at being invited to annotate *Snowbound*, first published in 1908, is twofold. First, aside from references to Byron's *Manfred*, with its witches and spirits, and the stage device known as the star trap, often employed for demon entrances, there is no supernatural catalyst within this collection of stories. It was, however, Gothic fiction that spurred the creation of the Dracula Society of London, which I co-founded with fellow actor Bernard Davies back in 1963. The Dracula Society attempted to lead like-minded individuals back to the books and away from the awful screen dramatisations that continue to spew forth.

Second, I have been able to unravel some of the mystique of theatre, for Bram Stoker was a theatre man for most of his adult life, business manager to the most modern actor manager of his day. Henry Irving was the first thespian to receive a knighthood (1895) for his contribution to the performing arts.

The theatrical stories in *Snowbound*, set between the middle of the nineteenth century and the book's publication are remarkable in their diversity. And they are assuredly semi-factual. There is little doubt that they are based on the Irving days and are therefore disguised portraits of those theatricals the author worked and toured with. In Volume II of *Personal Reminiscences of Henry Irving* Stoker records that in January 1904, while Irving was touring the USA and Canada, the company's train became 'snowbound' in the Adirondack Mountains in upstate New York. The experience evidently played on Stoker's mind, though in his fictional account he switches the setting from the United States to Scotland.

At least one of the constituent tales can also be traced to *Personal*

Reminiscences. The story 'Mick the Devil' surely owes its origins to floodwaters engulfing the touring company's train at Bayou Pierre, en route from New Orleans to Memphis in February 1896.

Snowbound offers much autobiographical comment. The Acting (that is 'business') Manager, Mr Wragge, utters the words '"all aboard"... after his usual custom' (page 26). Mr Wragge, 'who, being by needs of his calling a pushful person ... had become by a sort of natural selection ... Master of the Ceremonies' (page 29). Stoker here makes good-humoured jest of his own behaviour. Which, of course, leaves us with the Actor Manager himself, Mr Benville Nonplusser, surely based on Stoker's mentor. Henry Irving might have been 'nonplussed' by Stoker in their early years together. Or it might have been Stoker who was nonplussed by Irving. *Snowbound* was published three years after the great actor's death, and one cannot help wondering whether Stoker would have indulged in literary puns regarding his employer had Irving still been alive.

One might wish Stoker had given a richer physical description in these pages of his Actor Manager. Without them, the reader conjures images of Henry Irving, tall and spare with noble features, long hair falling to his shoulders, dressed in full frock coat with astrakhan collar, wide brimmed soft hat held correctly in his hand along with his silver-topped walking stick.

Irving's stature was equivalent to that of today's pop-stars, and he was received as 'Royalty' wherever he went. This is how Stoker presents Benville Nonplusser. The oral tales that emerge aboard the snowbound train pay homage to the spirit of theatrical professionals behaving (generally) honourably in trying circumstances.

After such a length of time it might be futile to play guessing games, but the temptation is strong. Is Miss Flora Montressor in *Snowbound* none other than Irving's Leading Lady, Ellen Terry? Who is the awful Tragedian, so full of classical rhetoric and self-importance? Stoker paints intimate scenes in large and small touring dates through the mouths of his characters and indulges his interest in local dialects to the point of confusion. Many a modern reader will share the frustration of the editor, even though Stoker's dialects are normally rendered in phonetic English. Such lapses are a recurring feature of Stoker's fiction, as those who have struggled with *Dracula*'s Mr Swales and Van Helsing will know to their cost.

Snowbound is remarkable both for its portrayal of disappearing types in live theatre, and of theatres themselves in the course of change at the beginning of a new century. And if Stoker writes with nostalgia, it is warm nostalgia without cant. He relates tales of touring theatre within the United Kingdom, the United States, and even Australia, which he never visited. As with his other fictional works, he lists real places, buildings and events, lending an air of authority, and then bemusing the reader by switching to names that are clearly invented.

One of the tales – 'A Star Trap' – leaves the assembled audience momentarily 'spell-stopped'. The horror of Stoker's tale still tightens the throat, even though 'Ma' ridicules it.

I have known many Ma's in Wardrobe. As a young man my father was a 'Super' in Henry Irving's Lyceum and in the 1950s I followed his footsteps into the theatrical world. I have echoed Stoker's touring days, performing everything from Shakespeare, to Melodrama, to 'Charley's Aunt'. I have played in many of the theatres named in *Snowbound*, for whom the only noticeable difference is the replacement of gas by electrics. In more recent years, of course, theatres have closed in abundance, falling from grace and used as bingo halls. *Snowbound* restores many precious memories.

I still warm to such days that only came to an end in the last decades of the twentieth century. Those Sunday gatherings at great railway stations like Manchester and Crewe, now sadly passed into theatre history, offered shared excitement – as was travelling itself at a time when actors wandered up and down the train seeking other travelling companies and sharing highlights and pitfalls of the week past. On Monday mornings one met with new stage staff. Every Monday night was opening night, for all parts of the country offered a different challenge. Audiences were 'alive', 'breathing' out there in the dark. One of Stoker's characters reminds us that in his day pre-theatre excerpts were performed out in the open streets, like 'trailers' in the cinema, to entice the public to full costumed performance within the theatre proper.

Stoker makes only one mention of a 'dresser', an essential if invisible figure attendant on leading performers, particularly those within poetic roles such as 'Manfred' and the Shakespearean classics. And although top stage staff are present – both the Wardrobe

Mistress and company Musical Director have their moment – the travelling maid-dresser of the Leading Lady is overlooked. In 1908 she would not have strayed far from her mistress, ever ready with the ubiquitous soothing tea in bone china cup.

What comes to light is the self-contained world of touring theatre around the turn of the century. Stoker would have known everything there is to tell about a travelling company. He supervised all the Lyceum's overseas tours, and in the first tour of the United States the company conveyed not only the actors but all scenery, costumes and equipment, much as is described in the tale 'A Moon-Light Effect'.

Such a huge undertaking would be economically impossible these days, not least the hiring of whole trains, complete with first, second and third class carriages. Few authors were as privileged as Stoker to be so active within the theatrical world. In *Snowbound* he shows his familiarity with *Pygmalion* (an earlier play than Shaw's immortal comedy of manners) and a play version of Jules Verne's historical romance *Michael Strogoff*, both now vanished in time.

Snowbound itself had almost vanished. Its re-birth is important for it is almost a biographical reference and comes from the pen of the only person who could describe the workaday life of the travelling Lyceum as it once was. In its pages I find little of creaking castle doors or black clouds scudding across full moons, but much of the delightful smell of grease paint that still acts as a narcotic to those once involved with it. To all of us who have ever been involved in the stage Stoker provides us with a cast of characters with which we can identify, and even to share some of the love-hate relationships experienced by the Irish writer.

What comes through on every page is an appreciation of theatrical childishness, the show-off behaviour, but always the ever-present camaraderie that ensures 'the show must go on'.

My thanks to Richard Dalby for supplying the original text for this edition and for his note on *Snowbound*'s bibliographical history; to David F Cheshire for checking theatrical references; and to Clive Leatherdale for editorial guidance.

Bruce Wightman
Founder President, The Dracula Society

1

The Occasion

FOR a little while the train seemed to stumble along amongst the snowdrifts. Every now and again there would be a sudden access of speed as a drift was cleared, just as in a saw-mill the 'buzz' saw rushes round at accelerated speed as the log is cleaved, or as a screw[1] 'races' when the wave falls away. Then would follow an ominous slowing down as the next snowdrift was encountered. The Manager,[2] pulling up the blind and peering out on the waste of snow, remarked:

'Nice cheerful night this; special nice place to be snowed up. So far as I can see, there isn't a house between the North Sea and the Grampians.[3] There! we've done it at last! Stuck for good this time!' – for the slow movement of the train stopped altogether. The rest of the Company waited in anxious expectancy, and it was with a general sigh of relief that they saw the door on the sheltered side of the saloon[4] open under the vigorous jerk of the Guard: anything was better than the state of uncertainty to which they had been reduced by the slow, spasmodic process of the last two hours. The Guard shook the rough mass of snow from him as he came in and closed the door.

'Very sorry to tell you, Ladies and Gentlemen, that we've come to a stop at last. We've been fighting the snow ever since we left Aberdeen,[5] and the driver had hopes we might win on as far as

---

1 propeller.

2 As no leading actor is mentioned, this is presumably the Actor Manager. Such a function was performed by Sir Henry Irving and the Lyceum Theatre, where Stoker was Acting (Business) Manager from 1878 to 1905.

3 The mountain range in central northern Scotland, for which Aberdeen is the closest port-city.

4 A first-class carriage, in this case, most probably reserved for the theatrical company for Sunday travel.

5 Aberdeen is the capital of the Grampian Region of Scotland, a port-city with a population of some 200,000. The theatre company have evidently been playing there. Stoker had a great fondness for this area, particularly Cruden Bay, 24 miles north of

Perth.[6] But these drifts are one too many for us. Here we are till daylight unless we can get some place nigh at hand for ye to shelter.' The practical mind of the Manager at once grasped a possibility.

'Why not go back to Aberdeen? We have cleared the road so far, and we should be able to run back over it now.' The Guard shook his head.

'That mecht do by ordinar';[7] but with a wind like this and such a snowfall as I've never seen the like of, we wouldn't be able to run a mile. But, anyhow, the Stoker[8] has gone out to prospect; and we'll soon know what to expect.'

'Tell the Driver to come here,' said the Manager. 'I should like to know exactly how we stand as to possibilities.' As the door opened for his passing out, the keen blast of icy air which rushed in sent a shiver through the whole Company. They were all too miserable and too anxious to say anything, so the silence was unbroken till the Guard returned with the Engine-Driver, the latter muffled, his black, oily clothes additionally shiny with the running of the melted snow.

'Where are we?' asked the Manager.

'Just about ten miles from anywhere, so far as I can make out. The snow falls so fast that you cannot see ten feet ahead, and the Stoker has come back, unable to get twenty yards away from the train.'

'Then I suppose there is no help for us till the storm ceases?'

'None!'

'And we have to pass the night on the train without any sort of comfort that you can give us?'

'That's so.' A groan from all followed the words. The Manager went on:

'Then we must do what we can to keep warm at least. We must

Aberdeen, where he set at least two of his fictional tales, and did much of the writing of *Dracula*, published in 1897.

6 Perth is a picturesque city in central Scotland, a popular touring destination, on the same rail link to London's King's Cross terminus. Queen Victoria customarily breakfasted at Perth on her way to Balmoral Castle by train.

7 'might do in ordinary circumstances.' Stoker's phonetic version of Lothian Scots.

8 This is unlikely to be an 'in' joke on Stoker's surname. Trains were coal burning at the turn of the 20th century, so required 'stoking'. Although a 'stoker' would not usually be spelt with a capital S, the author capitalises all occupations in *Snowbound*.

make a fire here.' The Guard struck in sharply:

'Mak' a fire in the Company's carriage, and burn the whole thing up to a cender?[9] Ye'll no mak' a fire here!' He spoke decisively. The Manager answered with equal decision:

'Who will prevent us?'

'I will.'

'Indeed! How will you do it?'

'By the authority of the Great North[10] line which I represent. So tak' ye formal notice that I forbid any fire in the carriage.' He paused, self-satisfied.

The Manager, taking his writing-pad from his pocket, wrote a few words. Then he said suavely:

'You understand I call on you as the representative of the Company to fulfil the Company's contract and leave us in London.'

'Ye know verra weel that I canna' do it.'[11]

'So you admit that, relying, I presume, on the common law of *force majeure*[12] to relieve you?'

'Aye!'

'Then read this paper; you see it is a formal notice. Now if you rely on *force majeure*, so do we; and we have a good deal more *force majeure* than you have! So here we'll make a fire, and, if need be, we'll fight your crowd in the doing of it. Brooke, you go to the workmen's carriage[13] and tell them to come here.'

The Call Boy[14] departed on his errand, and the Manager, seeing that the Guard had caved in, went on more genially:

'We'll not do any harm, as you shall soon see; but, anyhow, we don't mean to die like rats in a trap. Fire we must have, but we'll so arrange it that there will not be any harm done. All our people will

---

9 Stoker's interpretation of the vernacular - 'cender': cinder.

10 The Great North, or Great Northern Railway Line (GNRL), like all British railways at the time, was privately owned. It connected Aberdeen with Edinburgh, Newcastle-upon-Tyne, York and London, King's Cross.

11 'You know very well that I cannot do it.'

12 Bram Stoker was a qualified, but non-practising, barrister who littered his fiction with legal terminology. *Force majeure* means, depending on context, 'the wish of the majority', or 'circumstances beyond one's control'.

13 The leading players would travel first class, supporting actors second class, while the workman's carriage might even be third class.

14 Apprentice to the stage staff, sometimes an actor. He 'calls' the times from the half-hour to warn the artistes of the approach of 'Curtain-up'.

come in here, and your men can come also and share the warmth when we get it.'

'Aye! when ye get it,' murmured the Engine-Driver. The Manager smiled. 'You will see!' he observed. 'I shall stage-manage this. You may look on and get a wrinkle[15] for other snow-uppings.'

At this moment the door was torn open, and in rushed the half-dozen workmen, carpenters and property men, headed by the Master Machinist and the Property Master.[16] The rear was brought up by the Baggage Master.[17] The feet of all were clogged heavily with snow. The Manager spoke up just in time to prevent blows:

'Be quiet, men! We are snowed up, and will have to make ourselves comfortable as well as we can. We must make a fire here. Ruggles'[18] – this to the Property Master – 'can you get out any of the things from the vans?'

'Quite easy, sir! We're not loaded too full, and there is a clear way up the car.'

'And you, Hempitch?'[19] – this to the Master Machinist.

'Same, sir. We're not full either.'

'Very well! We must first make a fire in this carriage –' Here the guard broke in:

'Ye'll no mak' a fire here – except ower ma deid body.'[20]

'Hush, man!' said the Manager, holding up his hand. 'You'll see it will be all right. Just wait a while, and you will be satisfied; and then we shan't have to knock you on the head or tie you up. Now, Hempitch, you get out the thunder[21] and lay it here on the floor on the lee side of the car opposite this window; you will see, Guard, that the iron sheet will protect the floor. You, Ruggles, get a good

---

15 'wrinkle': a bright idea.

16 'Properties' are the furnishings and fittings of the stage. The Property Master and Master Machinist are responsible for 'mechanics' like 'vampire traps' and practical fireplaces, etc. Overall, lighting, particularly in the theatre, remained in 1908 by gas mantle or oil. Electricity was still in its infancy, especially with touring theatres.

17 The Baggage Master was in charge of costuming.

18 A possible pun, as 'Ruggles' would have distributed 'rugs' to the leading players on winter train journeys.

19 Perhaps another pun. Hemp ropes are used in scenery and are 'hitched' to cleats in the floor.

20 Over 'ma deid' (my dead) body. The Guard has a Lothian Scots accent.

21 A large hanging sheet of flexible metal that, when shaken backstage by the stage management, creates the sound of thunder.

lump of modelling clay from *Pygmalion*[22] and make a rim all round to keep in the ashes. Then, Hempitch, have half-a-dozen iron braces and lay them on billets[23] or a couple of stage boxes. On this platform put down one of the fireplaces – any one will do. Then, Ruggles, you will put a *Louis XI* chimney over it,[24] with a fire backing behind, and make an asbestos fire-cloth into a chimney leading out of the window; you can seal it up with clay. The Engine-Driver here will bring us some live coals from his engine, and one of the carpenters can take his saw and cut down a piece of the fence that I saw outside made of old sleepers.'[25]

The railway servants were intelligent men, and recognised the safety and comfort of the plan; so they went to the engine to get the live coals. When the workmen were bringing the coal, the Manager said to the Baggage Master:

'You had better bring in a couple of baskets of the furs from *Michael Strogoff*;[26] they will help to make us comfortable. And now, ladies and gentlemen, you had better produce your provisions. I see you have all hampers for the journey to London, and we can have supper. I have myself a big jar of Highland whiskey[27] and we shall have as jolly a time as we can.'

All was bustle, and though for a while the saloon was deathly cold whilst the various things ordered were being brought in, the extemporary fireplace was so quickly organised and the fire burned so well that warmth and comfort were soon realised. The Engine-Driver brought one or two appliances from his own store, notably a flat kettle, which, filled with melted snow, was soon hissing on the fire. The Property Master produced crockery from his professional

---

22 This cannot be the famous play by George Bernard Shaw, which was not written until 1913. Stoker seems to be referring to Greek mythology, as modelling clay is specified to create the statue that comes to life. Perhaps he has in mind William Brough's burlesque 'Pygmalion' (1867), or WS Gilbert's mythological comedy 'Pygmalion and Galatea' (1875).

23 Short thick wooden planks.

24 A Louis XI chimney was distinguished by its metal or stone canopy and was often situated in the middle of a room.

25 Sleepers are heavy ironwood logs laid down under railroad tracks.

26 A stage dramatised version of the historical romance written by Jules Verne in 1876, and which received several film treatments in the 20th century.

27 This Irish spelling of the famous Scots and Irish liquor might be a mistake. Though Stoker was Irish born, in Scotland the word is spelt 'whisky'.

stores; and supper began amidst the utmost comfort and good humour.

When it was done, punch[28] and tea were made and handed round, and pipes and cigars were lit. The Company, wrapped in furs, gathered as closely as they could get round the fire.

After a while the general buzz of conversation began to subside, and desultory remarks now and then marked the transition to absolute silence. This was after a while broken by the Manager with a sudden eruption of speech which seemed to awake the drowsy faculties of his companions.

---

[28] Punch in this context is whisky with a little sugar and hot water added.

2

A Lesson in Pets

'ONCE before, I spent some time with the Company in a saloon which was not altogether ideal.'

'Oh, do tell us about it,' said the Leading Lady.[1] 'We have hours at least to spend here, and it will help to pass the time.'

'Hear! hear!' came from the rest of the Company, who at least always seemed to like to hear the Manager speak. The Manager rose and bowed with his hand on his heart as though before the curtain,[2] sat down again, and began:

'It was a good many years ago – about ten, I should think – when I had out the No 1 Company of *Revelations of Society*. Some of you will remember the piece. It had a long run both in town and country.'[3]

'I know it well,' said the Heavy Father.[4] 'When I was a Leading Juvenile[5] I played Geoffroi D'Almontiere, the French villain, in the Smalls[6] in old George Bucknill's Company, with Evangeline Destrude as Lady Margaret Skeffington. A ripping good piece it was, too. I often wonder that someone doesn't revive it. It's worth a dozen of these namby-pamby – rot-gut-problem –'

---

1 The principal female player. The 'Star' of the company.

2 This would suggest that the Company Manager was also the Actor Manager, as was the case with Henry Irving. The leading actor, in fact, was used to making curtain speeches.

3 'town and country': London and the provinces.

4 The principal character actor.

5 The Leading Juvenile is the (usually) young romantic lead, for example, the younger brother, or Horatio in *Hamlet*. He is opposed to the Leading Man, who has the main part in the play and may be older. On occasion the two positions can overlap as actors may be sensitive about their actual ages.

6 'Smalls' were the lesser, or 'number two', touring dates. There were several categories of touring until the arrival of mass television in the 1950s broke the habit of going to see live theatre. The 'number ones' were the main centres of England, Scotland, Ireland (then still part of Britain) and Wales.

'Hush! hush!' came the universal interruption, and the growing indignation of the speaker calmed down. The Manager went on:

'That time we had an eruption of dogs.'

'Of what's?'

'How?'

'Of dogs?'

'How that time?'

'Oh, do explain!' from the Company. The Manager resumed:

'Of dogs, and other things. But I had better begin at the beginning. On the previous tour I had out *The Lesson of the Cross*,[7] and as we were out to rake in all the goody-goodies, I thought it best to have an ostensibly moral tone about the whole outfit. So I picked them out on purpose for family reasons. There were with us none but married folk,[8] and no matter how old and ugly the women were, I knew they'd pass muster with the outside crowd that we were catering for. But I did not quite expect what would happen. Every one of them brought children. I wouldn't have minded so much if they had brought the bigger ones that could have gone on to swell the crowds. I'd have paid their fares for them, too. But they only took babies and little kiddies that needed someone to look after them all the time. The number of young nursemaids and slips of girls from the workhouse[9] and institutions that we had with us you wouldn't credit. When I got down to the station and saw the train that the Inspector pointed out as my special, I could not believe my eyes. There was hardly a window that hadn't a baby being held out of it, and the platform was full of old women and children all crowing, laughing, and crying and snapping their fingers and wiping their eyes and waving pocket-handkerchiefs. Somehow the crowd outside had tumbled to it, and it being Sunday

---

[7] This was a well-known 'morality' play that followed the life of Christ.

[8] Having only married couples in the cast was designed to guard against impropriety. This was a hangover from the 'rogues, thieves and vagabond' image of theatre dating from the Middle Ages.

[9] As these girls came from institutions for the poor they were affordable even by touring actors, usually working for little more than their keep. Being 'in care', they also had a moral function to fulfil, and were usually required on stage to portray 'good' girls, with all that implied.

afternoon, they kept pouring in and guying the whole outfit. I could do nothing then but get into my own compartment and pull down the blind, and pray that we might get away on time.

'When we got to Manchester,[10] where we opened, there was the usual Sunday crowd to see the actors. When we came sliding round the curve of the Exchange[11] I looked out, and saw with pleasure the public anxiety to catch the first glimpse of the celebrated *Lesson of the Cross* Company, as they had it well displayed on our bills. But I saw run along all the faces in the line, just as you see a breeze sweep over a cornfield, a look of wonder; and then a white flash as the teeth of every man, woman, and child became open with a grin. I looked back, and there again was that infernal row of babies being dandled in front of the windows. The crowd began to cheer; I waited till they closed round the babies, and then I bolted for my hotel.

'It was the same thing over and over again all through that tour. Every place at which we arrived or from which we went away had the same crowd; and we went and came in howls of laughter. I wouldn't have minded so much if it did us any good; but somehow it only disappointed a lot of people who came to the play to see the crowd of babies, and wanted their money back when they found they weren't on. I spoke to some of the Company quietly as to whether they couldn't manage to send some of the young 'uns home; but they all told me that domestic arrangements were complete, and that they couldn't change them. The only fun I had was with one young couple who I knew were only just married. They had with them a little girl about three years old, whom they had dressed up as a boy. When I remonstrated with them they frankly told me that as all the others had children with them they thought it would look too conspicuous without, and so they had hired the child from a poor relation, and were responsible for it for the tour. This made me laugh, and I could say no more.

'Then there was another drawback from all the children; there

10 The industrial city of Manchester in north-west England remains a 'number one' touring date.

11 Sunday crowds used to assemble to admire the touring companies arriving or even passing through Manchester Exchange (junction) railway station, and these only really vanished with the rapid growth of television.

wasn't an infant epidemic within a hundred miles of us that some of them didn't get – measles, whooping-cough, chicken-pock, mumps, ringworm – the whole lot of them, till the train not only looked like a *crèche*, but smelt like a baby-farm and a hospital in one. Why, if you will believe me, during the year that I toured that blessed Company – and we had a mighty prosperous time of it, take it for all in all – the entire railway system of England was strewn with feeding-bottles and rusks.'[12]

'Oh, Mr Benville Nonplusser, how can you?' remonstrated the First Old Woman. The Manager went on:

'Just before the end of the tour I got all the Company together, and told them that never again would I allow a baby to be taken on any tour of mine; at all events, in my special trains. And that resolution I've kept from that day to this.

'Well, the next tour we went on was very different. It was, as I said, with the *Revelations of Society*, and, of course, the cast was quite different. We wanted to get a sort of toney, upper-crust effect;[13] so I got a lot of society amateurs to walk on. The big parts were, of course, done by good people, but all the small ones were done by swells.[14] It wasn't altogether a pleasant time, for there was no end to the jealousies. The society amateurs were, as usual, more theatrical than the theatricals; the airs that some of them gave themselves would make you laugh. This put up the backs of our own crowd – and they got their shirts out,[15] I can tell you. At first I tried to keep the peace, for these swell supers were mighty good and just what we wanted in the play; but after a bit it got to a regular division of camps, and I found that whatever I did must be wrong. Whatever one got or did they all wanted, and nothing was allowed to pass that gave even a momentary advantage or distinction to any of the

---

12 Fingers of bread baked hard as an aid for teething infants.

13 The baked and attractive top of a loaf of bread, so 'upper crust'. Hence the using of society amateurs in walk-on or minimal speaking roles. They quite often paid to tour for the prestige of appearing with a major company. This would have been especially so with the prestige of Irving's Lyceum.

14 Expensively dressed, against the ordinary working man's coarser garb.

15 Taking jackets off freed the clothing ready for fisticuffs. Stoker is perhaps recalling his 'Donegal Fair' days in Dublin.

crowd. By-and-by I began to have to put my foot down, but every time I did so there was a kick somewhere; so I had to be careful lest I should have no one at all to play the piece.

'I seemed never to be able to get an hour's rest from some of the jealousies that were constantly springing up. If I could have managed to forestall any of them it would have been easy enough, but the worst of it all was that they were perpetually breaking out in a new place; and it was only when it was too late to do anything to prevent a row that I came to know the cause of the one then on.

'Having forbidden babies on the former tour, I did not think it was necessary to forbid anything else; and the consequence was that I suddenly found that we had broken out in an eruption of Pets. My Leading Lady then, Miss Flora Montressor, who had been with me on seven tours and was an established favourite all over the Provinces, had a little toy wheaten terrier that she had taken with her everywhere since ever she had been with me. Often other members had asked my Acting Manager if they too might bring dogs; but he had always put them off, telling them that the railway people didn't allow it, and that it would be better not to press the matter, as Miss Montressor from her position was a privileged person. This had always been enough with the regular Company, but the new lot had all of them got pets of some kind, and after the first journey, when their attention had been called to the irregularity, they simply produced dog-tickets,[16] and said they would pay for them themselves. That was enough for the other lot, and before the next journey came there wasn't a soul in the whole crowd but had a pet of some kind. Of course, they were mostly dogs – and a queer lot they were, from the tiniest kind of toy up to the biggest sort of mastiff. The railway people weren't ready for them – it would have taken a new kind of van for them all – and I wasn't ready for them either; so I said nothing then. The following Sunday I got them all together, and told them that after that journey I was afraid I could not permit the thing to go on. The station was then like a dog-show, and I could hardly hear myself speak for the barking and yelping

---

16 For a small fee it was permissible to bring a pet into the compartment (in this case a saloon carriage reserved for the cast of the Tour Company). Otherwise the animal was confined to the guard's van.

and howling. There were mastiffs and St Bernards, and collies and poodles and terriers and bull-dogs and Skyes, and King Charleys and dachshunds and turnspits – every kind of odd illustration of the family of the canine world. One man had got a cat with a silver collar, and led it by a string; another had a tame frog; and several had squirrels, white mice, rabbits, rats, a canary in a cage, and a tame duck. Our Second Low Comedy Merchant[17] had got a young pig, but it got away at the station, and he hadn't time to follow it up. When I spoke to the Company they were silent, and they all held up their dog-tickets – all except Miss Flora Montressor, who said quietly:

'"You gave me leave years ago to bring my little dog."

'Well, I saw that nothing could be done then except with the kind of row that I didn't want. So I went to my own compartment to think the matter over.

'I soon came to the conclusion that an object-lesson of some kind was required; and then a bright idea struck me:

'"I should get a pet myself."

'We were then bound for Liverpool,[18] and early in the week I slipped down to my old friend Ross, the animal importer, to consult with him. In my early days I had had to do with a circus, and I thought that on this occasion I might turn my knowledge to account. He was out, so I asked one of the men if he could recommend me some sort of pet that wouldn't be pleasant for a nervous person to travel with. He wasn't a humorous man, and at once suggested a tiger. "We have a lovely full-grown one," he said, "just in from Bombay. He's as savage as they make 'em. We have to keep him in a place by himself, for when we put him 'in a room with any of the others, he terrifies them so that they are like to quit in a body."

'I thought this cure might be too drastic, and I didn't want to close my tour in a cemetery or a gaol, so I suggested something

---

17 The Low Comedians held a special place right up to Henry Irving's day, when he introduced a lower key method acting that did not cater for extemporisation. Irving was rare, at that time, in playing Shakespeare's Shylock for real, not as a Low Comedian with exaggerated nose and red 'fright' wig.

18 Liverpool, on the River Mersey, acts as a cross-over port to Dublin, and has a big Irish community.

milder. He tried me with pumas, leopards, crocodiles, wolves, bears, gorillas, and even with a young elephant; but none of them seemed as if it would suit. Just then Ross himself came in, and took me off to see something new.

'"Just come in," he said; "three ton of boa-constrictor from Surinam.[19] The finest lot I've ever come across." When I looked at them, although my early training had somewhat accustomed me to such matters, I felt a little uneasy. There they lay in cases like melon-beds, with nothing over them but a glass frame, with not even a hasp[20] to hold it down. A great slimy, many-coloured mass all folded about and coiled up and down and round and round; – except for a head sticking out here and there one would have thought that it was all one big reptile. Ross saw me move a little, so he said, to reassure me:

'"You needn't be skeered.[21] This weather they're half torpid. It's pretty cold now, and even if the heat were to get at them they wouldn't wake up." I didn't like them, all the same, for whenever one of them would give a gulp, swallowing whatever food he was on at the moment – a rat or a rabbit or what not – the whole mass would stir and heave and writhe a little. I thought how nice a lot of them would look amongst my crowd; so there and then I agreed with Ross to hire a lot of them for the next journey. One of his men was to come down with my workmen to Carlisle, whither we were bound, to take them back again.

'I arranged with the railway company to have for that journey one of their large excursion saloons, so that all the members of the Company would have to travel together instead of going into separate compartments grouped in parties. When they gathered at the station none of them were satisfied. There was, however, no overt grumbling. I had casually mentioned, and the word had gone round, that I was coming with them myself,[22] and had prepared a treat for them. That they evidently expected something in the way

19 A large non-poisonous snake that kills by compression, here from Dutch Guyana in South America. Stoker returns in spirit to the land of the vampire bat. The boa constrictors are here measured by weight, not by numbers.

20 Clasp passing over a staple and secured by a pin.

21 Stoker cannot resist the local dialect for 'scared'.

22 'Coming with them myself' suggests he usually has a private compartment to himself.

of a picnic was manifested by the frequent inquiries of some of them from the porters and the Baggage Master as to whether my personal luggage had arrived. I had carefully arranged with Ross's people that my contribution was not to be brought till the last moment, and I had privately tipped the Guard and asked him to be ready for an immediate start after its arrival. The special train had been scheduled for a quick run, and was not to stop between Liverpool and Carlisle.

'As the starting time drew near, the Company took their places as they had secured them in the saloon, the first comers getting to the furthest ends. The carriage became by a sort of natural selection divided into two camps. The dogs belonging to either side were in the centre. When "all aboard"[23] had been called out by my Acting Manager after his usual custom, the last of the Company took their places. Then a heavy truck came quickly along the platform, surrounded by several men. It contained two great boxes with unfastened lids, and as there were many hands available these were quickly lifted into the saloon. One was placed opposite the door on the off-side of the carriage, and the other put just inside the door of entry, which it blocked.

'Then the door was slammed and locked; the Guard's whistle sounded, and we were off.

'I needn't tell you that all this time the dogs were barking and howling for all they were worth, and some of them were only held back by their owners from flying at each other. The cat had taken refuge on a hat-rack, and stood growling, with her tail thickened and lashing about. The frog sat complacently in its box beside its master, and the rats and mice were nowhere to be seen in their cages. When the baskets came in some of the dogs cowered down and shivered, whilst others barked fiercely and could hardly be held back. I got out my Sunday paper[24] and began to read quietly, awaiting developments.

'For a while the angry dogs kept up their clamour, and one of them, the mastiff, became almost unmanageable. His master called

---

23 The Acting Manager usurps the functions of the station master on the platform, this being a private carriage.

24 It was the habit to read the Sunday papers on tour. They offered the chance to read any reviews of the shows and to catch up on world events.

out to me:

'"I can't hold him much longer. There must be something in that box that upsets him."

'"Indeed!" I said, and went on reading. Then one or two of the Company began to get alarmed; one of them came over and looked curiously at the box, bent close and sniffed suspiciously, and drew back. This whetted the curiosity of others, and several more came around and bent down and sniffed. Then they began to whisper amongst themselves, and one of them asked me point-blank:

'"Mr Benville Nonplusser, what is in that box?"

'"Only some pets of mine," I answered, without looking up from my paper.

'"Very nasty pets, whatever they are," she answered tartly. "They smell very nasty." To which I replied:

'"We all have our fancies, my dear. You have yours and I have mine; and since all you belonging to this Company have your pets with you, I have determined to establish some of mine. You'll doubtless grow to like them in time. In fact, you'd better begin, for they are likely to be with you every journey henceforth."

'"May we look?" asked one of the young men. I nodded acquiescence, and as he stooped to lift the lid the rest gathered round – all except the man with the mastiff, who had his hands full with that clamorous beast. The young man raised the lid, and as he saw what was within, threw it back as he recoiled, so that it fell over, leaving the whole interior exposed. Then the crowd drew back with a shudder, and some of the women began to scream. I was afraid that they might attract attention, as we were then nearing a station, so I said quietly:

'"You had better be as quiet as you can. Nothing irritates serpents so much as noise. They think it is their opportunity for seeking prey!" This bold statement seemed to be verified by the fact that some of the boa-constrictors sleepily raised their heads with a faint hissing. Whereupon the crowd simply tumbled over each other in their efforts to reach the further corners of the saloon. By this time the man with the mastiff was becoming exhausted by his struggling with the powerful animal. As I wished to push home my lesson, I said:

'"You had better keep those dogs quiet. If you don't, I shall not answer for the consequences. If that mastiff manages to attack the serpents, as he is trying to, they will spring out and fight, and then –" I was silent, for at such a point silence is the true eloquence. The fear of all was manifested by their blanched faces and trembling forms.

'"I'm afraid I can't hold him any longer!" gasped out the man.

'"Then," said I, "some of your companions who have dogs also should try to help you. If not, it will be too late!" So several others came, and by the aid of their rug-straps[25] they managed to tie the brute securely to a leg of the bench. Seeing that they were nearly all half-paralysed with fright, I lifted the lid to the top of the box again; at which they seemed to breathe more freely. When they saw me actually sitting on the box, something like a far-off smile began to glow on the countenances of some of them. I kept urging them to keep the animals quiet; and as this was a never-ceasing work, they had something to occupy them.

'I was a little nervous myself at first, and had any of the boa-constrictors knocked his head against the lid of the box I should have made a jump away. However, as they remained absolutely tranquil, my own courage grew.

'And so some hours passed, with occasional episodes, such as when some one of the many pets would make a disturbance. The singing of the canary, for instance, was resisted with angry curses. But the vials of the wrath of all were emptied forth at its owner when the hitherto silent duck began its homely song, "Quack, quack!"

'"Will you keep that blasted brute quiet?" came an angry whisper from the worn-out owner of the mastiff. Upon which a good many of those on whom time had had a quieting effect smiled.

'When my watch told me that we were within a short distance of Carlisle, I stood upon the box and made a little speech:

'"Ladies and Gentlemen, I trust that the episode of to-day, unpleasant though it may have been, will not be ultimately without beneficial effect. You have learned that each one of you owes something to the general good, and that the selfish pursuance of

---

25 There was no proper heating on trains. Most sensible travellers carried personal travelling rugs, which were rolled and secured by a strap.

your own pleasure in small ways has sooner or later to be accounted for. When I remonstrated with each of you as to this animal business, you chose to take your own way, and even went so far as to reconcile your personal and sectional jealousies in order to unite against me. I therefore thought that I would bring the difficulty home to you in a striking way! Have I done so?"

'For a while there was silence; and then a smile and a faint affirmative answer here and there, so I went on:

'"Now I hope you will all take it in as good part as I have taken all that went before. Anyhow, my mind is made up. Pets shall be included with babies in the *Index Expurgatorius*[26] of our tour. In the meantime, for the remainder of this tour, if anyone else brings pets, so shall I; and I think you know that I know how to choose my own. Anyone objecting to this can cancel the engagement right here. Has anyone got anything to say?" Some shrugged their shoulders, but all were silent; and I knew that my victory was complete. As I was stepping down, however, I caught Miss Montressor's eye as tearfully she looked at me and then at her little dog, so I added:

'"This does not apply to Miss Montressor, who years ago had permission to take her dog. I shall certainly not deprive her of that privilege now."

'And not a soul objected.'

'Next!' said the Acting Manager, Mr Wragge, who, being by the needs of his calling a pushful person, usually took such prominent responsibilities as were unallotted or unattached, and who in the present instance had become by a sort of natural selection, manifested by tacit consent of the Company, Master of the Ceremonies.

There was dead silence, for the séance was as yet so young that no one seemed to wish to be put forward. The keen-eyed MC recognised the situation at a glance, and, turning to the Leading Lady on the Manager's left, said:

'You'll have to go on next, Miss Venables. The turn will travel with the wine – if we had any for it to travel with.' The hint was not lost on the First Low Comedian, who promptly unscrewed the top

---

26 Pets and babies were banned. One wondered how the Latin was interpreted by the lesser educated.

of his flask and gallantly pushed it, together with a tumbler and the water-bottle, in front of the blushing girl. 'Here is the wine,' he said; '*vin du pays*.'[27] She made a gentle motion of protest, but the Manager poured a small portion of whiskey in the glass, together with a fair supply of water. She acknowledged the courtesy with a pretty little bow, and then turned an appealing eye round the Company. 'I will with pleasure do what I can for the public good,' she said, 'but I am really and truly at a loss to know what to tell. My life has not yet been a very adventurous one, and I don't know anything worth telling that has ever happened to myself.'

One of the Young Gentlemen, who secretly admired her from afar, blurted out:

'I know something which would interest us all.'

'What is that?' asked the MC quickly. The Young Man blushed and stammered as he answered, looking apprehensively at the object of his devotion, who gazed at him inquiringly with bent brows:

'It was some joke – something – I don't know what it was – that they had in the *Her Grace the Blanchisseuse*[28] Company just before I joined them. Someone had sworn them all to secrecy, so no one would tell me why it was that they always spoke of Miss Venables as "Coggins's Property."'

The girl laughed merrily. 'Oh, I did that. It was too funny altogether. I didn't mind it myself; but there was another; poor Coggins, who was an excellent fellow, took to heart so much the perpetual chaff of the Company that he sent in his resignation. I knew that he had a wife and family, and would not leave a good situation unless he was really hurt; so I made a personal request to everyone, and they all promised not to tell how the name came to be. But I am not bound, so if you like I will tell you; for the thing is all over long ago, and Coggins is a prosperous builder in the Midlands.'[29]

---

27 The wine of the country, a typical Low Comic joke.

28 'Blanchisseuse' translates as 'washerwoman', hence 'Her Grace the Washerwoman'. This, of course, is the name of the play on tour and not the owner of the company. It appears to be a parody of Sardou and Moreau's comedy 'Madame Sans Gêne' – presented at the Lyceum in April 1897 – with Irving as Napoleon and Ellen Terry as his washerwoman.

29 The central counties of England, comparatively remote from the sea, with cities such as Birmingham, Coventry, Leicester.

'Hear! hear!' came from all, for their expectations were aroused. So the Leading Lady began:

3

Coggins's Property

'WHEN I was in *Her Grace the Blanchisseuse*, I had just gone on the stage and played a lot of little parts of a line or two.[1] Sometimes I was a body without a voice, and sometimes a voice without a body!'

'*Vox et præterea nihil*,'[2] murmured another Young Man, who had been to a public school.[3]

'Amongst the voice parts was one which was supposed to come from a queen who was in bed in a room off the salon which was represented in the scene. The edge of the bed was dimly seen, and I had to put out a hand with a letter and speak two lines. My attendant took the letter, the door was shut – and that was all. Of course, I had not to dress for the part, except that I put on a little silk and lace jacket, and one sleeve as of a nightdress, so I used to come on from the side just before my cue and slip into, or, rather, on to the bed. Then a property man came with a quilt embroidered with the Imperial Arms, which he threw over me, tucking in the edge nearest the audience. The man originally appointed to this work was Coggins, and as he had a great deal of work to do – for it was a "property" play[4] – he only got to me in time to do his work and clear out before the door opened and my attendant came in. Coggins was an excellent fellow, grave, civil, punctual, sober, and as steady and stolid as a rock. The scene was a silent one, and what appeared to be my room was almost in the dark. The effect to the audience was to see through the lighted salon this dim sleeping chamber; to see a white hand with a letter emerge from the bed

---

1 Pieces of dialogue.

2 'A voice followed by nothing.'

3 'public school': the British term for a private school.

4 A play with numerous items for the actors to handle as part of the plot, for example, daggers, goblets.

curtains, and to hear a drowsy voice as of one newly roused from sleep. There was no opportunity of speaking a word, and no need for it. Coggins knew his work thoroughly, and the stage manager and his assistants insisted on the most rigorous silence. After a few nights, when I found Coggins so attentive in his work, I said "goodnight" when I passed him at the stage-door, and gave him a shilling.[5] He seemed somewhat surprised, but doffed his cap with the utmost respect. Henceforward we always saluted each other, each in our own way; and he had an occasional shilling, which he always received with a measure of surprise. In other portions of his nightly work and mine I often came in contact with, or rather in juxtaposition to, Coggins; but he never seemed to show the same delicate nicety which he exhibited towards me in his manipulations of my tucking-up in *Her Grace the Blanchisseuse.* The piece, as you know, had a long run in London, and then the original Company went round the "Greats"[6] for a whole season. Of course, the Manager took with him all the people who worked in London who were necessary, and amongst them came the excellent and stolid Coggins.

'After months of work done under all possible conditions, we all came to know our cues so well that we were able to cut the time pretty fine; we often turned up at our places only at the moment of our cues. My own part was essentially favourable for this, and I am afraid I began to cut it a little too fine; for I got to arriving at my place just a second or two before Coggins made his appearance with the Imperial quilt.

'At last one night, in the Grand at Leeds[7] – you know what a huge theatre it is, and how puzzling to get on the right floor – I went just across the line of safety. I was chatting in the dressing-room with Birdie Squeers, when the call-boy came tearing along the passage shouting: "Miss Venables, Miss Venables. You're late! Hurry

5 Pre-decimal British coinage. Twenty shillings equalled one pound sterling. The 'Queen's Shilling' was the amount paid to each soldier who joined the Army. At the turn of the 20th century you could buy a fair meal for a shilling.

6 The First Cities of England, Scotland and Ireland.

7 Leeds is the principal city of what was then called the West Riding of Yorkshire. The Grand was one of several fine theatres of Leeds, but is the only one still standing today.

up, or there will be a stage wait!"[8] I jumped for the door and tore along the passage, and got to the back of the stage just in time to meet the stolid Coggins with his stolidity for once destroyed. He had the Imperial quilt as usual folded over one arm, but he was gesticulating wildly with the other. "'Ere!" he called in a fierce whisper to a group of the other workmen. "Who the 'ell has took my Property?"

"'Yer property!" said one of the others. "Garn! ye juggins. Hain't ye got it on yer arm?"[9]

"'This! This is all right," he answered. "That ain't what I mean. Wot I want is wot I covers up with this."

"'Well, and ain't the bed there? You keep your hair on, and don't be makin' a hass of yerself."[10] I heard no more, for I slipped by and got on to the bed from the back. Coggins had evidently made up his mind that his particular work should not be neglected. He was not responsible for the figure in the bed, but only for putting on the quilt; and on the quilt should go. His look of blank amazement when he found that the quilt did not lie flat as on his first effort amused me. I heard him murmur to himself:

"'A trick, is it? Puttin' the Property back like that. I'll talk to them when the Act's over."[11] Coggins was a sturdy fellow, and I had heard him spoken of as a bruiser, so I thought I would see for myself the result of his chagrin. I suppose it was a little cruel of me, but I felt a certain sort of chagrin myself. I was a newcomer to the stage, and I had hitherto felt a sort of interest in Coggins. His tender, nightly devotion to his work, of which I was at least the central figure, had to me its own romantic side. He was of the masses, and I had come of the classes,[12] but he was a man and I a woman, and a man's devotion is always sweet – to a woman. I had

---

8 An embarrassing, inexplicable onstage silence that tells the audience something has gone wrong. If held to blame, the offending actor may well be fined.

9 'Garn! ye juggins': 'Go on, you beer jug. Haven't you got it over your arm.'

10 Keep your hair on refers to the old belief that in distress your hair fell out. 'Don't make an ass out of yourself.' The accent portrays Coggins as a Londoner, probably from the East End.

11 Most plays, then and now, were divided up into three acts or sections, with an interval between each for refreshments out front and scenery changes on stage.

12 The Leading Lady confirms that Coggins was uneducated, whereas she was middle class and well-schooled.

often taken to heart Claude Melnotte's[13] romantic assumption of Pauline's reply to his suit:

"That which the Queen of Navarre[14] gave to the poor Troubadour:
"Show me the oracle that can tell nations I am beautiful."

'But it had begun to dawn upon me that my friend and humble admirer, Coggins, had no interest in *me* at all. My part in the play came to an end before the close of the scene, and so when the doors were closed I slipped from my place as usual; I did not, however, go to my dressing-room as was my habit, but waited to see what Coggins would do. In his usual course he came and removed his quilt; and again there was a look of annoyed amazement on his face when he found that it lay flat on the bed. Again he murmured:

'"So they've took the Property away again, have they? We'll see about it presently." When he had removed the Imperial quilt two other men came, and as usual lifted away the bed, the Empress's bedroom being opened no more during the play. As there was no more to be done till the play was over, I went to the stage-door, ostensibly to ask if there were any letters for me, but in reality because the workmen usually assembled there when not wanted on the stage, and it was here that I expected the *dénouement*. Several of the carpenters and property men were smoking[15] outside the stage-door, and to them presently came Coggins, thoroughly militant in manner.

'"Now, you chaps," he said, "there's somethin' I want to know; an' I mean to 'ave it, stryte[16] 'ere! Which of you's 'avin' a lark with me?"

'"Wot jer' mean?" said one of the others with equal truculence. He was a local man, and certainly looked like a fighter. "Wot are ye givin' us?"

---

13 Melnotte was the hero, played by Henry Irving at the Lyceum, of Edward Bulwer Lytton's *The Lady of Lyons*. Irving's Leading lady, Ellen Terry, played Pauline.

14 Former Kingdom in south-west Europe established in the 9th century by the Basques. Navarre is today divided between Spain and France.

15 This is the reason for the gathering. Most Victorian theatres were built basically of wood, so smoking was not allowed backstage.

16 'stryte': straight.

Coggins, recognising an antagonist worthy of consideration, replied as calmly as he could:

'"Wot I want to know is 'oo's a plyin' tricks with my Property?"

'"What property, Coggins?" asked one of his own pals.

'"Yer know as well as I do; the one wot I covers up on the bed with that quilt." There was a roar of laughter from the men, and a hail of chaff began to rain on him.[17]

'"Oh! if that's your property, Coggins, I wonder what your missis will say when she hears it!"

'"Why, that ain't no property; it's a gal."

'"Well, boys, when the divorce is asked for we can prove that there weren't nothin' 'atween 'em. When old Jeune[18] 'ears that he didn't know the differ between a property and a gal, he'll up and say, "Not guilty. The prisoner leaves the Court without the slightest stain on his character."'

'Coggins grew very pale and perplexed-looking, and in a changed voice he asked:

'"Boys, is this all a cod[19] or what?"

'"Not a bit of a cod," said one. "Do ye mean to say that you didn't know that what you tucked up every night was one of the young ladies?"

'"No!" he answered hotly. "'Ow could I know it? I never come on except just in time to put on the quilt and tuck it up. It was nearly dark, and it never said nothin'! An' 'ow the 'ell was I to know the bally thing was alive!" This was said with such an air of sincerity that it broke me all up, and I burst into laughter. Coggins turned angrily round, but, seeing me, took off his cap with his usual salute.

'"That's yer Property, Coggins!" said one of the men; and Coggins was speechless.

'Of course, he was unmercifully chaffed, and so was I. Various members of the Company used to come up to me on all sorts of occasions, and, after gazing into my eyes and touching me, would say in a surprised way:

'"Why, the bally thing's alive!"

---

17 'chaff': the husks of grain. Here, a medley of witty comments in unison.

18 'old Jeune'. The old Judge or Magistrate in a Civil Court.

19 'cod': in this context, a hoax.

Coggins appeared to have a rough time of it with some of the others. For weeks he never had less than one black eye, and not only were most of our own men in a similar condition, but we left behind us wherever we went quite a crop of contusions. I knew it was no use my saying anything on my own account, for you might as well ask the wind to leave the thrashing-floor alone as for a parcel of friends to drop a good subject of chaff; but after a while I had to take pity on poor Coggins, for he sent in his resignation. I knew he had a wife and family, and that as his situation was a good one he would not leave it unless hard pressed. So I spoke to him about it. I think that his explanation had, if possible, more unconscious humour in it than his mistake. But there was pathos, too, and Coggins showed himself to be, according to his lights, a true gentleman.

'"There's two things, Miss, that I can't get away from. My missis is a good ole sort,[20] and takes care of the kids beautiful. But she believes that there ain't in the world only one Coggins – I'm him; and as I 'ave to be away so much on tour she gets to thinkin' that there's other wimmin as foolish as herself. That makes her a bit jealous; an' if she was to 'ear that I was every night a-tuckin' up a beautiful young lady – savin' your presence[21] – in a bed, she would give me Johnny-up-the-orchard.[22] An' besides, Miss – I hope you'll forgive me, but I want to do the right thing if I can – I've not give up carpenterin' and took to the styge without learnin' somethin' of the ways of the quality.[23] I was in the Dook o' York's Theatre[24] when they had a ply[25] what showed as how in high society if a man gets a girl into any trouble, no matter how innocent, but so as how she's chaffed by her pals, he's got to marry her to put it right. An', ye see, Miss, as how bein' married already I couldn't do the right thing ... so I've resigned, and must look for another shop."'

''Ow would a dead byby suit you to hear on?' asked the Sewing

---

[20] 'missis': wife. 'ole': old.

[21] 'savin': 'with respect of your presence'.

[22] Chased up the orchard.

[23] 'the quality'. 'The humble and the quality', that is, Coggins and Miss Venables.

[24] 'Dook (Duke) o' York's', famous still among London theatres.

[25] 'ply': play.

Woman, with an interrogative glance round the company. 'I know of one that was simply 'arrowing.' The ensuing silence was expressive.

No one said a word; all looked at the fire meditatively. The Second Low Comedian sighed. In a half-reflective, half-apologetic way she went on, as if thinking aloud rather than speaking:

'Not that I know overmuch of bybies, anyhow, never havin' 'ad none of my own, though that's partly due that I was never married. Any'ow, I never 'ad the chances of some – married or onmarried.'

The Wardrobe Mistress, known in the Company as 'Ma,' here felt it incumbent on her, as the ostensible matron of the party, to say something on such a theme:

'Well, bybies is interesting things, alive or dead. But I don't know whether they're the cause of most noise alive or dyin' or dead. Seems to me that we've got to have it out either in screaming or sobbing or mourning, whatever you do. So, my dears, it's just as well to take things as they come, and make the best of them.'

'You may bet your immortal on that!' said the Second Low Comedian. 'Ma's head is level!' With the instinct of the profession, they all applauded the 'point,' and Ma beamed round her. Applause given to herself was a rare commodity with her.

'All right! then we'll drive on,' said the bustling MC. 'You choose your own topic, Mrs Wrigglesworth – or, rather, *Miss* Wrigglesworth, as I should say after your recent confession of spinsterhood.' The Sewing Woman coughed, cleared her throat, and made those other preparations usual to the inexperienced speaker. In the pause the Tragedian's deep voice resounded:

'Dead babies are always cheerful. I love them on the walls of the Academy.[26] The Christy Minstrels'[27] deepest bass as he trills his carol, *Cradle's Empty; Baby's Gone*, fills me with delight. On such a night as this, surrounded as we are by the profound manifestations of Nature's feller forces, the theme is not uncongenial. Methinks the very snow-wreaths with which the driving tempest smites the

---

26 The Royal Academy of Arts, Piccadilly, London.

27 The Christy Minstrels were the brainchild of Edwin P Christy (1815-1862) and came to fame performing the works of Stephen Collins Foster (1826-1864) in the USA. Their popularity was such that after his death they toured the USA and Europe, including London.

windows of our prison-house are the beatings of dead baby fingers as they clamour to lay ice-cold touches on our hearts.' The Company, especially the women, shuddered, and the comments were varied.

'Lor'!' said the Wardrobe Mistress.

'Bones!' – the slang name of the Tragedian – 'never beat that in his nach.[28] He'll be wanting to have a play written round it,' said the Low Comedian. The Tragedian glared and breathed hard, but said nothing. He contented himself with swallowing at a gulp the remainder of his whiskey-punch.

'Refill the Death Goblet!' said the Second Low Comedian in a sepulchral voice. 'Here, Dandy' – this to the Leading Juvenile – 'pass the whiskey.'

The servile desire to please, habitual to her, animated the Sewing Woman to proceed on her task:

'Well, Mr Benville Nonplusser,' she began, 'and Lydies and Gentlemen, which I 'opes you'll not expect too much from me in the litery way. Now, if it was a-sewin' on of buttons – no matter wherever placed! An' many a queer tale I could tell you of them if I could remember 'em, and the lydies wouldn't object – though blushes is becomin' to 'em, the dears! Or if I could do summat with a needle and thread, even in a 'urry in the dark and the styge a-waitin' of –' She was interrupted by the Low Comedian, who said insinuatingly:

'Go on, my dear. This ain't the time nor place for one to object to anything. The ladies' blushes will do them good, and will make us all feel young again. Besides' – here he winked round at the Company – 'the humour, conscious or unconscious, of the various situations with which your episodical narrative must be tinged will give an added force to the gruesomeness which is attendant on the defunct homunculus.'[29]

'You are too bad, Mr Parmentire,' whispered the Singing Chambermaid to him. 'If she makes us blush you will be responsible.'

'I accept the responsibility!' he answered gallantly to her, adding *sotto voce* to the Prompter: 'And I won't need any cut-throat insur-

---

28 'nach': natural life.

29 'homunculus': a little man, dwarf.

ance at Lloyd's to protect me against that hazard.' The Sewing Woman went on:

'Well, as to the dead byby, which it makes me cry only to think of it, and its poor young mother growin' colder and colder in spite of 'ot poultices –'

Her voice was beginning to assume that nasal tone which with a woman of her class is at once a prelude to and a cause of tears. So the Manager promptly interrupted:

'We're simply in raptures about that baby; but as an introduction to the story, couldn't you give us some personal reminiscence? The baby, you see, couldn't be your own, and therefore it can only be a matter of hearsay –'

'Lor' bless you're 'eart, sir, but I ain't 'ad anythink to reminisce.'

'Well, anything you've seen or heard in the theatre. Come now, you've been a long time in the business; did you never see anything heroic happen?'

'As 'ow, sir, 'eroes not bein' much in my way?'

'Well, for instance, have you never seen a situation saved by promptness, or resource, or daring, or by the endurance of pain –'

'Oh, yes, sir. I seen them things all in one, but it wasn't anythink to do with the dead byby.'

'Well, just tell us first how it was, and how resource and readiness and the endurance of pain saved the situation.'

As the Manager spoke he glanced around the Company with a meaning look; so she proceeded:

4

The Slim Syrens

'THE first show what I ever went out with was Mr Sloper's Company for the *Society Gal,* what was called "The Syrens."[1] You see, when the play was first done, society 'ad long wysts[2] and thin 'ips and no bust to speak of, and the lydies what plyed in it original was chose according. My! but they *was* a skinny lot – reg'lar bags o' bones; if ye'd a biled down the lot for stock you'd no need to 'ave skimmed it. W'y, the tights they wore! – Speakin' of legs as yards of pump-water ain't in it; theirs looked as you might 'ave rolled 'em up on a spool. And as to their chestys – why, you might 'ave put 'em through the mangle and none ever the wuss – except the mangle from jerkiness, where it might 'ave well expected to take it a bit india-rubbery. But the ply 'ad so long a run that the fashion got changed, and the swells began to like 'em thick. So the gals got changed, too; some of 'em makin' up with 'eavy fleshings[3] an' them shove-up corsets, what'd take a pinch out of your – your stummick an' swell out your throat with it, till they come into line with the fashion. Lor', the things I've seen the girls do to make theirselves look bulkier than what nature made 'em! Any'ow, when they 'ad run the fust companies twice round the Greats, Mr Sloper thought as 'ow 'e'd go one better on the fashion. "Ketch the risin' tide" was ever 'is mortar![4] So the company engyged for "*The New Edition Society Gal*" was corkers![5] They used to say in

---

1 In this tale Stoker allows the narrator, Miss Wrigglesworth, to exploit phonetic dialect, as in the title. The legendary Sirens (sea-nymphs, half-woman, half-bird) lured passing ships to their death. Only Odysseus was able to hear their song, tied to the mast of his ship, while the rest of the crew's ears were stopped with wax. The Wardrobe Mistress's English is again London 'Cockney'.

2 'wysts': waists. 'plyed': played. 'biled': boiled. 'chestys': chests. 'wuss': worse. 'stummick': stomach. 'Lor': Lord. 'fust': first.

3 'fleshings': padded pink tights.

4 'Catch the rising tide was ever his motto.'

5 'corkers': eye-catching. Cheap wine or spirits came with screw-on tops. Those with 'cork' stoppers signalled a vintage collection. The company engaged was therefore a reputable one.

the wardrobe as 'ow there was a twenty-stun[6] standard, and no one would be engyged that couldn't pass the butcher. Of course, the wardrobe of the theayter or the travelling shows was no use for "The Slim Syrens" – for that's what they came to be known as. We 'ad to 'ave a lot of tights made a purpose, and when they come 'ome the young man 'as brought 'em laughed that much that he cried, and he wanted to stay an' see 'em put on, till I 'unted 'im out.[7] I never see such tights in all my time. They was wove that bias everywhere as I felt my 'eart sink when I thought of 'ow we was to take up ladders in 'em; for fat girls does a deal more in that wy than slim ones – let alone the 'arder pullin' to drag 'em on. But the tights wasn't the wust. You remember, Mrs Solomon,[8] as 'ow there's a scene when Society goes in for to restore Wat-ho,[9] and the 'ole bilin'[10] dresses theirselves as shepherds. Mr Sloper didn't want to spend no more money than he could 'elp; so down he goes to Morris Angel's,[11] tykin' me and Mrs Beilby, that was wardrobe mistress to the Slim Syrens, with 'im. Well, ole Morris Angel trots out all the satin britches as 'e 'ad in stock. Of course, the most of 'em was no use to our little lot, but we managed to pick out a few that was likely for lydies what runs large. These did for some of the crowd, and, of course, the principals got theirs made to order.[12] They wasn't so much fuller than Angel's lot, arter all; for our lydies, though bulky, liked good fits, and sure enough at the dress rehearsal most of them looked as if they had been melted and poured in. Mr Sloper and the styge manager and some of the syndicate gentlemen[13] what came to see the rehearsal had no end of fun, and the things they said, and the jokes they made, and the way that the girls run after 'em and 'ammered of 'em playful,[14] as girls does, 'd made you laugh to have seen it. And talk of blushin'! Well,

---

6 Cattle are stunned before slaughter at the abattoir. The girls' appearance left the viewer 'stunned'.

7 'hunted him out.' Threw him out of the Wardrobe area.

8 Mrs Soloman and Miss Wrigglesworth may be the same person.

9 'to restore Wat-ho'. To restore normality.

10 'the whole biling (boiling)'. That is, everybody.

11 Morris Angel's costumiers in London is still operational.

12 The costumes of the Stars are always individually tailored.

13 Investors in the show.

14 Punched them playfully.

there! The most particular of the lot, and him what didn't like the laughin' and the jokin', was Mr Santander, that was going to take out the Company as manager - him what they called "Smack"[15] Santander in the green room. There was one girl what was his lady-friend as he had put into the lead, though the other girls said as 'ow she 'ad no rights to be shoved on that way. But, there! Gals is mostly like that when another gal gets took up and 'elped on. Why, the things what I've 'eard and seen just because a girl was put into the front row![16] When she was bein' dressed, which it was in the wardrobe, because Mr Santander was that particular that Miss Amontillado should be dressed careful, well do I remember the remark as Mrs Beilby made: "Well, Miss," says she, "there's no denyin' of that you *are* very fine and large!" Which was gospel truth, and no concealin' of it either in the wardrobe or on the styge, an' most of all in the orchestra,[17] where the gentlemen never left for their whiskey-and-soda, or their beer or cards or what not, or a smoke, till she 'ad gone to 'er dressin'-room, which most of 'em got new glasses - them what didn't use opery-glasses.[18] Well, when dress rehearsal[19] was over, Mr Sloper 'e tried to be very serious, and, says he, "Lydies, you must try and be careful; remember that you carry weight!" - which that hended 'is speech for 'im, for he choked with laughter till the syndicate gentleman come and slapped 'im on the back, and then laughed, too, fit to bust.

'When we was startin' the season Mr Santander sent for me and spoke to me about Miss Amontillado, and told me that it was as much as my plyce was worth[20] if anything went wrong with 'er. I told 'im as 'ow I'd do my best, and I took Miss Amontillado[21] aside, and, ses I, "Miss, it's temptin' providence it is," says I, "for a fine, strapping young lydy as you in britches like them," I says. "You do kick about that free," I says; "and satin is only satin at the best, and

15 A 'bottom-slapper', apparently.

16 The front row of the chorus, which is most conspicuous to the audience.

17 The front rows directly behind the orchestra pit, where those who came to ogle had the closest seats.

18 Opera glasses. Short-range binoculars to allow close study of the performers.

19 Final rehearsals in full costume.

20 She would be fired if anything went wrong.

21 Miss Amontillado. Stoker's drinking taste, perhaps. Amontillado is a rare quality Sherry immortalised in Poe's Gothic tale 'The Cask of Amontillado.'

though the stryn is usual on it in the right direction up and down, there's the stryn on yours all round.[22] What if I was you I wouldn't take no chances," I says. Well, she laughed, and says she, "Well, you dear old geeser"[23] – for she was a young lydy as was alwys kind and affable to her inferiors[24] – "and what would you do if you was me?" "Well, miss," I says, "if I was as gifted as you is, I'd have them made on webbin' what'd 'old, and wouldn't show if the wust come to the wust." She only laughed, and gave me sixpence, and, says she, "You're a good ole sort, Sniffles" – for that's what some of the young ones called me – "and I'll tell Smack how well you look after me. Then perhaps he'll raise your screw."

'Both Mr Santander and Miss Amontillado was anxious about the first night, and there was bets in the dressin'-room as to how she'd come off in 'er 'igh-kickin' act. You'll remember, Mrs Solomon, 'ow the ply goes, as 'ow to the surprise of all, the young Society gal as didn't do nothin' more nor a skirt-dance, sudden ups and tykes the kyke[25] from all the perfeshionals. When Miss Amontillado was dressed for the act in her shepherd dress, I says to her, "Now miss," I says, "do be keerful"; and Mr Santander 'e says, "'Ear! 'ear!" 'e says. "Oh, I'm all right," she says. "Look 'ere, Smack," and she ups and does a split as made my 'eart jump, it was that sudden, and up on her 'eels agin afore you could say Jack Robinson![26]

'Well, just then I 'eard the Call-Boy a-comin' down the passidge 'ollerin', "Miss Amontillado! Miss Amontillado!" "'Ere!" she says; and as he came into the room she puts 'er 'ands over 'er 'ead and

---

22 The 'stryn' (strain) on her breeches would be caused by her 'high kicking'! These 'Syrens' danced rather than sang, so this was a real problem to 'Ma', with her job 'on the line'.

23 'Geeser', usually spelled 'geezer'. A geyser is a sporadic fountain of hot subterranean water, from Old Norse 'to gush'. Hot water in bathrooms – produced by gas jets – was a luxury at the turn of the 20th century. 'Geeser', by extension, is an old, bubbling, gushy, eccentric character – in London slang an affectionate compliment.

24 This was not necessarily a put-down of herself. Ordinary folk have often been accused of inverted snobbery, 'knowing their place' and being proud of it.

25 Takes the cake – taking precedence over the professionals. In this case it refers to doing the 'splits', the spread-legged leap down to the floor, one leg forward, one behind, in the Can-Can.

26 Boxer Jack Robinson was famous for quick knock-outs; hence the term means 'immediately'.

does a sal-lam that low that 'er back 'air nigh swept the floor. And lo and behold! as she bent I 'ears a 'ideous crack; and there was 'er back up and down in two 'alves as you'd 'ave put a sweepin' brush atween.

'"Now you've done it, Miss," I says; and there was she laughin' and cryin' all in a moment, for it weren't no joke to 'er to 'ave her big scene queered[27] like that the fust time as she done it. And there was Mr Santander a-tearin' at 'is 'air – which there wasn't none too much of it – and 'im a-bullyin' of 'er dreadful, and sayin' as 'ow 'e'd cancel 'er engygement – which 'e weren't no gentleman, that 'e weren't. And all the time the Call-Boy yellin' out, "Miss Amontillado, there'll be a styge wyte!"[28] and 'im fit to bust laughin'. Impident[29] young monkey! I knew as 'ow if anything was to be done it must be done quick, so I whips out a big sailmaker's needle what we sewed canvas with and the tapes on the stair-treads, an' a lot of wax-end twine as I kep' for fixin' reefs in the ballet shoes;[30] for it wasn't no child's play as to them britches with a fine gal like that, and them so tight. I tried to get a holt of the two sides of the tear to bring 'em together; but, lor' bless you! the reef was that wide I couldn't get 'em close any'ow. The dresser that was in with me, she tried to 'elp; but it weren't no use. And then Mr Santander 'e kem and 'ad a try, but it weren't no go. Then I tykes the Call-Boy by the 'air of 'is 'ead and mykes 'im ketch 'old too, 'im bein' a bicyclist and 'is fingers that 'ard. Then the gas-man came to 'elp with two sets of pinchers; but all we could do we couldn't make them sides of that split meet.

'We was all in despair and the time goin' by; we could 'ear the 'ootin' in front at the wayt, and the styge-manager kem tearin' along, yellin' and cursin' and shoutin' out, "What in 'ell is wrong? Where is the bally girl? Why don't she 'urry up?"

'At that very moment a hinspiration came to me. It was a hinspiration an' nothink else, for there was that there poor gal's success at styke, much less 'er situation. "'Ere," say I, "my dear, just

---

27 To ruin or spoil.

28 'Stage wait' but this time because of the exposure of Miss Amontillado.

29 'Impident': impudent.

30 All 'pointe' shoes for dancers are sewn over the toe area to prevent 'reefs' – splitting of the silk material.

you lie down on the sofy on yer fyce, with yer bust on the cushing and yer toes out with yer 'eels in the air." She sor in a flash what I were up to, and chucked 'erself on the sofy, and the Call-Boy shoved a bolster under 'er instep. My! but she bent up double that 'ard that I 'eard the webbin' of the abominable belt as she wore go crack.

'But, lydies and gents, the situation was saved; the roos[31] was a pernounced success. Them two distant hedges kem[32] together like twins a-kissin', and afore you could say "Boo!" I 'ad my needle and was a-sewin' of 'em up that firm. I was in such a 'urry that some of the stitches took in the skin as well as the satin. But she was a plucky gal, and tho' she 'owled, she didn't wriggle away. There wasn't no time to cut the thread, and as soon as the last stitch was in she jumps up, tearin' the stitches through her skin, and bounds out on the styge with the needle 'anging' be'ind. Mind you, 'er blood was up, and she landed on to the styge like a good 'un.

'The roar that come from the Johnnies[33] when they see 'er was good to 'ear!

'But this is nothin' to do with what I was goin' to tell you about that story of the dead byby –'

'Oh! blow the dead baby,' said the Second Low Comedian. 'Put it in a bottle and keep it on the shelf till called for. After an act of living valour like what you've told us, we don't want anything dead.'

'Next!' said the MC, in the pause that ensued.

The Low Comedian being next in order had been gradually becoming more ill at ease as his own time approached; it was manifest that in the armoury of his craft was no weapon suited to deal with a necessity of extempore narration. Some of those on whom he was accustomed to sharpen his wits knew, either instinctively or by experience, of this weakness, and commenced to redress or avenge whatever they might have suffered at his hands. They began by

---

31 'roos': ruse.

32 The two edges came together.

33 Stage Door Johnnies. The 'Orchestra' oglers who afterwards wait their chance at the artistes' entrance to take the girls out to a champagne and oyster supper – and high hopes.

encouragement, outwardly genuine and hearty, but with an underlying note of irony which could not fail to wound a spirit sensitive on the point of its own importance:

'Buck up, old man.'

'Drive on, Gags.'

'Have a drink first. You're always funnier afterwards.'

'What do you mean by that?' asked the indignant Low Comedian, fiercely. 'What do you mean by "afterwards"? Do you mean when I'm drunk, or have had too much, or what?'

'Only a joke!' said the Prompter, in a deprecatory way, for his was the unhappy remark. The Heavy Father who was usually one of his butts struck in:

'He probably meant that you were funnier in your intention after the opportunity of being funny had existed as a fact.' The Low Comedian did not see his way to a fitting reply, so he replied to the arrow with a stone:

'Indeed! If I was you, old man, I would try Irish! It's sometimes hard to understand you through Scotch!'

'Time!' cried out the MC, anxious to prevent what looked like the beginning of a quarrel. The bottle, or I should say the Tribune, rests with Mr Parmentire.' The Low Comedian looked at the fire reflectively for a few seconds; then he passed his hand through his hair, and after glaring all round the Company, began:

'I suppose you know, Ladies and Gentlemen, that there is a current idea that a Low Comedian must be always humorous.' He was interrupted by the Tragedian, who, prefacing his remark with a Mephistophelean Ha-ha-ha![34] said:

'If there is, it is a mistake; or, at best, an exploded idea. Surely, humour is the last quality to be expected from a Comedian, let alone a Low Comedian. But, of course, I may be prejudiced; I never took much stock of the horse-collar[35] myself!'

'Si-lence! Si-lence!' said the watchful MC in the manner of a Court crier, whilst the Leading Juvenile whispered to the Prompter:

---

34 A protracted stage laugh that implies menace or mischief. Here we surely have a wryly humorous reference to Sir Henry Irving, who was famous for his interpretation of the demon Mephistopheles in the dramatic version of *Faust* and in Stoker's first novel, *The Primrose Path*.

35 One of the 'props' in scenes of rustic humour.

'Bones got in at him for the dead baby fingers that time.' The Low Comedian went on:

'Well, if humour in private life is expected, it's not always to be had, as Bones has very properly implied in his best knock-down-and-drag-out manner,[36] however we may deceive the public by our arts and utterances in public.

---

[36] 'unsubtle'. The Low Comedian was physical in his humour so, literally, 'knocked down and dragged his *foil* offstage'. Nowadays such humour is largely confined to 'Brokers men' in Christmas Pantomime, Circus clowns, or north country Vaudevillians, though it has also become popular in Hollywood comedies and alternative comedy. At the turn of the 20th century it was gratefully accepted by a less sophisticated audience, especially up in the 'gallery', and was essential for 'front cloth' work while the next full scene was being changed behind it.

5
A New Departure in Art

'I REMEMBER once being called on to be humorous under circumstances which made me feel that fun was as difficult to catch as a bat with a fishing rod.' With the cultivated instinct of listeners, which all actors must be able to pretend to be, the Company gave simultaneously that movement of eagerness which implies a strained attention. The perfection and simultaneity of the movement was art, but the spirit of truth lay behind it, for all felt whatever was coming was real. The Low Comedian, with the trained instinct of an actor, felt that his audience was with him – *en rapport* – and allowed himself a thought more breadth in his manner as he proceeded:

'I was playing "Con" in *The Shaughraun*[1] for want of a better, having been put into the part because I could manage a kind of brogue. We had a wretched Company, and we went to wretched places, places nearly bad enough to do us justice. At last we found ourselves in a little town on the west side of the Bog of Allen.[2] It was hopeless business, for the people were poor; the room we played in was an awful hole, and the shebeen[3] which they called a hotel where we all stayed was a holy terror. The dirt on the floor had caked, and felt like sand under your feet. As to the beds –'

'Oh, don't, Mr Parmentire; it's too dreadful!' said the Leading Lady, shuddering. So he went on:

'Anyhow, the audience – what there was of them – were fine. They weren't used to play-acting, and I think most of them took what they saw as reality – certainly while the curtain was up. We played three nights; the second night when I came out a big-made

1 This is a reference to one of the great Irish plays of the 19th century. Dionysius Boucicault's 'The Shaughraun' (1874) is regularly revived today.

2 Vast peat bog between the Lilley and Shannon rivers in West Meath.

3 A place that serves alcohol, probably with an earth floor in the bar area. A low inn.

young man came up to me and said:

'"Kin I have a wurrd wid ye, sorr?"[4]

'"Begob! but ye may," said I, in as near a brogue as I could get to his. "Twinty av ye loike!"[5]

'"Then whisper me," said he, and, taking me by the arm, he led me across the street where we were alone. "What is it?" I asked.

'"I seen ye, sorr, at the wake[6] to-night. Begorra, but it was an illigant toime.[7] Shure the fun iv that would have done good to a rale[8] corpse, much less to his frinds. I wondher now wud ye care to do a neighbourly act?" He said, this with considerable diffidence. There was something genial and winning in his way, as there is generally with Irishmen; so I said as heartily as I could that I hoped I would, and asked him how I could do it. His face brightened as he answered:

'"Well, there's a wake to-night, a rale wake, yer ann'r, at Kenagh beyant and the widdy[9] is in a most dishtressful state intirely. Now, av yer ann'r as is used to the divarshins iv wakes[10] would come, shure it might help to cheer her up. It's only a rough place, surr, an' the byes an' the girrls is all there is; but there's lashins iv whiskey an' tobaccy,[11] an' wan iv the quality like yer ann'r will be mighty welkim."

'That did it! For a man who took me for one of the quality I would have done anything! I tell you, you have to be mucking about for a spell in such places as we had been, and treated with the contempt which used to be the actor's meed[12] in his private life in such places in my young days, to appreciate fully the help such a thing was to one's self-esteem. I told my pals that I was going to a local party, for I didn't want to disturb my new dignity all at once, and went off with my friend. We went on a donkey cart without

4 'Can I have a word with you, sir?' Stage Irish by Dublin-born Stoker.

5 'By God but you may. Twenty if you like.'

6 A Wake is the watch over the dead the night before burying. An Irish funeral.

7 'Begorra ... illigant toime': By God ... elegant time.

8 'rale': real.

9 'yer ann'r': your Honour. 'Kenagh beyant': no known place. 'widdy': widow.

10 'divarshins iv wakes': funeral differences.

11 An Irish Wake is heavy on hospitality, with whiskey and tobacco provided in abundance.

12 'meed': reward, due praise.

springs.[13] Such a cart, and such a road! There was a bundle of straw to sit on, so I was comfortable enough; except when the jolting through an unusually deep rut banged me about more than was consistent with physical self-restraint. At last we stopped where a small house stood back some hundred yards from the road. The light was coming through the little windows and the open door, that seemed quite bright through the inky blackness of the night. I separated myself from the straw as well as I could, and got down. A small boy appeared out of the darkness, like an attendant demon, and took away the donkey and cart. It seemed to fade into space, for, as it disappeared through a gap in the hedge, the wheels ceased to sound upon the soft turf. My friend said:

'"Stiddy, surr! the boreen[14] is a bit rough!" He was right; it was! I stumbled towards the house through what seemed the bed of a small watercourse floored with peculiarly uneven boulders. When we got near the house, the light from within told more on the darkness, and as we came close to the projecting porch, the white oblong of the open doorway to the right became darkened as a figure came out to meet us – an elderly woman with grey hair and a white cap and a black dress. She curtsied when she saw my dress, and said with a certain air of distinction that most Irish-women have in their moments of reserve, and which all good women have in their grief:

'"Welkim, yer ann'r. I thank ye kindly for pathernisin' this house iv woe!"[15]

'"God save all here!" said my cicerone as he removed his caubeen.[16]

'I repeated the salutation, feeling a little bit chokey about the throat as I followed the woman into the house.

'The room was a good-sized one, for it was no peasant's hut I was in, but a substantial farmhouse. Seated about it were some thirty or forty people of both sexes, old and young. Nearly all the

---

13 This is called a jaunting cart in Ireland, and the driver a 'Jarvy', who is traditionally a fine teller of tales to those on board.

14 'Steady, sir!' A boreen is an unmade lane no more than a cart's width.

15 'Welcome, your honour. I thank you kindly for patronising this house of woe.'

16 'my guide as he removed his cap'.

men were smoking, some short cutty pipes[17] as black as your hat, others long churchwardens,[18] which manifestly came from a batch which lay on a table beside a substantial roll of "Limerick twist."[19] The tobacco was strong, and so were the lungs of the smokers, so the room was in a sort of thick haze, which swayed about in visible wreaths whenever a passing gust drove in through the open door. There was a huge fire of turf[20] on the hearth, over which hung a great black kettle puffing steam like a locomotive. The air was fragrant with whiskey punch,[21] of which some great jugs were scattered about. The guests drank from all kinds of vessels of glass, crockery, tin, and wood, each of which seemed *pro bono publico,*[22] for they were attacked at times by those nearest with the utmost impartiality. As there was manifestly not seating room for so many people, a good many of the women, old as well as young, sat on the men's knees in the most matter-of-fact way and with the utmost decorum.

'My cicerone, who was on all sides saluted as "Dan," took a pipe from the table and filled it. One of the girls, shifting from her living stool, took a blazing turf from the fire with the tongs, and held it to him as a light. He then helped himself to punch from the nearest vessel, looking round the room and repeating the salutation: "God save all here!"

'The widow herself pressed me into an armchair, vacated for the purpose by a powerful-looking young man who had been sitting with a girl on each knee. She then handed me a steaming jorum[23] of punch in one of the few glass tumblers which she had wiped with

---

17 'cutty': cut from clay. It was the custom to supply pipes as well as tobacco at a funeral.

18 A 'churchwarden' is a long-stemmed clay pipe.

19 'Limerick twist' tobacco was shipped from America since Elizabethan times and prepared in the town of Limerick (famous as the birthplace of the Limerick rhymes) on the River Shannon.

20 Turf (peat) was the common fuel of the Irish countryside, dug out with a flat spade, then dried in squares of semi-carbonized vegetable matter. Many old Irish farmhouses and inns still use it.

21 Whiskey, honey and hot water.

22 Indiscriminately used.

23 An individual jug, usually called a 'iurach'. A measure of yew wood, broad at the base and narrow at the neck. It seems doubtful Stoker had much fluency in the native language. He probably learned his Irish from his mother, who was born in Sligo on the Atlantic coast of Ireland.

the corner of her apron before filling it. She also gave me a pipe and tobacco, and brought me herself a sod of turf with which to light it when filled. This was the evident courtesy to a stranger, which, through all her grief, was a duty not to be overlooked.

'Nearly all those present seemed cheerful; some of them laughed, and I could not but feel that the instinct and purpose of the occasion was to counteract in some way the gloom and grief which were centred round the black coffin which rested on two chairs in the centre of the room. I could not myself but feel moved and solemn as I looked at it. The lid was laid on loosely, slightly drawn down so as to show the dead face[24] which lay, still and waxen, within. A crucifix of black wood with the Figure in white lay on the coffin lid, together with some loose flowers, amongst which a bunch of arum lilies stood out in their white beauty.

'I think I really needed the punch to brace me up, for there was something so touching in the whole affair – the deep-felt grief held back with so stern a purpose, the sympathy of so many friends, all giving what comfort they could with their presence, combating the chill of death with the warmth of living and loving hearts – that it almost broke me up. It was evident that they had had some music, for a flute lay on the table, and a set of bagpipes stood in a corner. I sat quiet and waited, for I feared that, in my ignorance, I might jar on some feeling of those afflicted, either by some sin of commission, or of omission. I felt a little uncomfortable occupying a chair all to myself when every other seat in the place did double or treble duty; and I found myself beginning to speculate whether some of the girls would come and sit on *my* knee. But they didn't.'

'Showed their good taste!' said the Tragedian with a saturnine smile as he reapplied himself to his toddy.

'That's just it, Bones!' answered the Low Comedian sharply, 'showed their good taste! Remember that these weren't the pot-house rabble that you are accustomed to. They were decent, respectable folk, who could be familiar enough with one another without any ill thought of their neighbours or themselves, but they

---

[24] This practice is normal in Celtic communities. The departed one is not regarded as fully gone until the actual burying. At the 'Wake' he 'enjoys the company!' The open coffin is also common in East European funerary rites.

wouldn't lower themselves by a like familiarity with strangers, especially when they had any mistaken idea that their guest belonged to the quality.'

'Anyhow, they showed their good taste, whether according to Bones's idea or mine, and so I sat in solitary grandeur, and was by degrees fetched up to the level of the acceptance of fact by the whiskey punch. The restraint of the presence of a stranger wore away shortly, and I listened with interest to some of the music, quaint old airs with a lilt in them, and always an underlying note of pathos. This was especially manifest in the bagpipes, for the Irish bagpipes so far differs from the Scotch that it produces a softness of tone impossible to the other. You do not know, perhaps, that the Irish pipes have half-notes, whilst the Scotch have only full ones.'[25]

Here a sort of modified snort was heard in the immediate neighbourhood of the Musical Director, and a remark was made, *sotto voce,* in which the words 'grandmother' and 'eggs' were distinguishable. The Low Comedian turned a swift glance in the direction, but said nothing, and, after a pause, went on:

'Presently Dan got up and said:

'"Widdy, this gintleman here is the funniest wan that iver I seen. Maybe now ye wouldn't mind av he was to give us a taste iv what he can do?"

'The Widow gravely nodded as she replied: "Shure, an' av his ann'r will pathernise us so far, we'll all be grateful to him. What like kind iv fun, Dan, does his ann'r consave?"[26] I felt my heart sink. You know I'm not bashful.'

'You're not! not by a jugful!' interrupted the Tragedian. The Low Comedian smiled. He understood, from the low 'h-s-s-h' that ran through the saloon that the audience were with him, so he reserved his repartee, and went on:

---

[25] Traditional Scottish bagpipes are blown with the mouth with martial intent, while Irish bagpipes are played with bellows for strictly melodic purposes. There exists good humoured dispute over who invented them.

[26] 'does his Honour prefer?'

'Not as a general rule, but there is a time for everything, and here, in the very presence of death, perpetually emphasised to me by the light of the candles which surrounded the coffin, flickering through the smoke, levity seemed out of place. Dan's chuckle of laughter as he began to speak almost disgusted me:

'"Oh, byes, but he's the funny man entirely. I seen him to-night play-actin', an' I thought I'd laugh the buttons from aff iv me britches."[27]

'"What did he do, Dan?" asked one of the girls.

'"Begob, but he reprisinted a corpse. 'Twas the most comical thing I iver seen."[28] He was interrupted by a violent sobbing from the widow, who, throwing her apron over her head, sat down beside the coffin, one hand leaning over till it touched the marble cheek and rocked herself to and fro in floods of tears. All her self-restraint seemed broken down in an instant. Some of the younger women sympathetically burst into tears; and the scene became almost in a moment one of unmitigated grief.

'But the very purpose for which the wake is ordained is to combat grief and its more potent manifestation. The stronger and more experienced spirits in the room looked at each other, and prompt action was taken. One old man put his arm round the widow, and with a fair use of force, raised her to her feet and led her back to her seat by the chimney corner, where she rocked herself to and fro for a little, but in silence. Each "boy" who had a crying girl on his knee, put his arms round her and began to kiss and pet and comfort her, and the crying soon ceased. The old man who had attended to the widow said, in a half-apologetic way:

'"Don't mind her, neighbours! Shure, 'tis the ways iv weemen[29] when their hearts is sore. It's hard, it is, for the poor souls to bear up all the time, an' yez mustn't be hard on thim when they're bruk down.[30] It's different wid us min!"[31] There was an iron resolution in the man's bearing, and a break in his voice which showed me that

---

27 'from off my trousers'. A variation of 'burst my breeches'.

28 'My God, but he represented a corpse.' One of the merriments at an Irish Wake is to literally leap over the coffin.

29 'it is the ways of women'.

30 'bruk down': broke down.

31 'with us men'.

he was one of those whose self-control was accomplished with effort. "Who is he?" I asked from the man sitting next me.

'"Shure, an' he's the brother iv the corpse, surr!" came the answer. The apologetic words were received with a series of sympathetic nods and shakings of the head and muttered words of acquiescence:

'"Thrue for ye!"

'"Begob, but that's so!"

'"Weemin is only weemin, afther all!"

'"The poor crathur; God be aisy wid her in her sorra!" In the midst of this, Dan went on just as if nothing had happened. That he was right in his endeavour was shown by the brighter look on the faces of all as he resumed:

'"'Twas the funniest thing I iver seen! He was the corp himself, and him not dead at all. Tear an ages! but that was a quare wake intirely. Wid the corpse drinkin' the keener's[32] punch whiniver she nodded her head." Here the keener, sitting on a low stool on the side of the coffin away from the fire, hearing through her somnolence the implied slight to her function, woke on the instant, and, with a half-angry look at the speaker, said: "Keeners doesn't sleep – not till the words is said over the grave." Then, as if to show that she herself was wide awake, she raised a keene which, beginning low and sad, rose and rose in pitch and volume till the rafters seemed to buzz and ring with the mournful sound. Thenceforth, and throughout the remainder of the night, she keened at intervals, generally choosing such times as the interruption of the current proceedings would bring into prominence the importance of her lugubrious office. No one, however, considered her professional labours as an interruption, but went on just as if nothing were occurring. It was embarrassing at first, but after awhile no more interrupted one than the ticking of a clock or the whistling of the wind, or the rush and clash of waves. Dan proceeded:

'"Thin he tuk the shnuff, an' threw it in the faces iv the polis."[33]

'"An' what did he do that for, wastin' it on the likes iv them?"

---

32 'keener': semi-professional wailing mourner.

33 'tuk the schnuff': took the snuff. Powdered tobacco sniffed up the nostrils, much favoured by the landed gentry of Britain and the 'small folk' of Ireland. 'iv the polis': of the police. Police were never much in favour with the Irish countryfolk.

asked a fierce-looking old woman.

'"To make them incapable, for shure!"

'"Make them incapable! Wid shnuff! Wid shnuff!" she said with fine scorn. "Musha,[34] but that's not the way I'd make the polis incapable – more'n they are already. It's wid a blackthorn[35] on their skulls, an' plenty iv it at that!" There was a slight pause, which was broken by an old woman, who said in a conversational way:

'"Who'd a thought, now, that there was that comicality in a wake? Musha, but I've been attindin' them for half a hundhred years, an' I niver seen a funny wan yet."

'Dan at once championed his own choice.

'"Maybe, acushla,[36] that was because this gintleman wasn't the corpse on the occasion. Av he had a-been like I seen him the night, it's houldin' in yer stummick wid laughin' ye'd be!"[37]

'"Corpses does be ginerally sarious[38] enough!" remarked an old man. "I'm thinkin' it's grateful we'd be to wan what'd give us divarshion iv any kind." Dan didn't seem to like these interruptions. There was something of the spirit of the impresario in him, and he manifestly wished to exploit what he considered his funny-man addition to the entertainment, so he began to explain:

'"Musha! but won't yez undhershtand that this wasn't a real corp, but a man what was only purtendin' to be wan.[39] It was play-actin' and his ann'r is the funniest man I ivver seen."'

'Limited opportunities have very dreadful effects!' murmured the Tragedian; but no one took any notice. The Low Comedian proceeded:

'Dan turned to me and says he: "Wudn't yer ann'r do somethin' funny?"

'"Good God!" I said, "I couldn't be funny in the presence of the dead – it wouldn't be respectful!"

---

34 'Musha': a flexible exclamation. In this case, 'Indeed!'

35 a walking stick or club (shillelagh) made of blackthorn.

36 'acushla': darling or sweetheart.

37 'holding your stomach with laughing'.

38 'ginerally sarious': generally serious.

39 'purtendin to be wan': pretending to be one.

'"Put that out iv yer mind, surr," said the brother of the corpse; "shure, all these frinds an' neighbours is here out iv respect, an yet they does what they can to cheer up the poor widdy woman[40] that has but little to comfort her in her sorra. It's well, so it is, to help her to forgit!" This was so manifestly true that I bowed to the occasion, and said that I would do what I could to amuse them. I would just take a minute to think of something, if they would pardon me. With true Irish delicacy they began to talk to each other, ostensibly letting me alone as I wished. Dan smiled round with the consciousness that his efforts were about to be crowned with success, and remarked for the general good:

'"Begob, there was wan quare thing,[41] at the wake I'm tellin' yez iv – all the girrls on the flure wint wan afther th'other[42] an' kissed the corpse!" There was a murmur of incredulous astonishment from all, and many whisperings and strugglings between the girls and the men who held them on their knees.

'"That wouldn't do you, Katty!" remarked one young man to the girl beside him, but her retort came pat, "It'd be a good custom for you, avick,[43] for the only chance you'd iver get in yer life is whin ye're dead." Then there was a pinch unseen, and a most manifest smack on the man's face which would have given a less hardy person a headache for a day. It was evident that conversation was being made on my account, for the next remarks kept on the subject of me and my work.

'"Begob! but play-actin' is a mighty curious thing intirely!" said a man. "I seen some iv it wanst at a fair in Limerick. Shure, they was hins that was play-actin',[44] an' cute enough they wor."

'"I seen a man wan time at Ballinasloe Heifer Fair turnin' music out iv a box, an' him wid a monkey dhressed up like a gineral!"[45]

'"An' I seen dogs what would climb up a laddher an' purtend to be dead, an' would jump as high as yer head through a hoop. I wonder, surr," this to me, "if ye would jump a bit through a hoop.

---

40 'widdy woman': widow.

41 'By God, there was one strange thing.'

42 'the girls on the floor went one after the other'.

43 'avick': I think.

44 'there were hens play-acting'.

45 'with a monkey dressed up as a general'.

Mind ye, it's a mighty divartin' thing to luk at,[46] an' would do the widdy a power iv good."

'I really could not stand this; it was too damned humiliating – our Art compared with the antics of a hen, a monkey, and a dog, as if we were all comrades of equality. But it was all meant in so kindly a way that I made up my mind to sing a comic song. I gave them "Are you there, Moriarty?"[47] for all I was worth. Artistically, it was a success, though, the subject being a glorification of police, was, I felt after I had begun, deplorably inappropriate. They were a splendid audience, and after I had begun to entertain them, I felt I could depend on them thoroughly, so played with the thing, and did it as well as I could. But at first it was dreadful to stand up there looking down on the dead man in his coffin, and facing the widow with her swollen eyes, with the crucifix and the flowers and the death-lights right under me to try to be comic. It was the ghastliest thing I ever knew, or that I ever shall know. I felt at first like a fiend and a cad and a villain and a scoffer, all in one. In fact, I may say that in that awful moment I realised what it must be to be a tragedian! It was only when I saw the apron slowly drawn from the face of the widow, and her poor, worn eyes brightening up perceptibly through her tears, that I began to understand how salutary was the purpose of the wake. Finally, I gave them "Shamus O'Brien"[48] as a recitation, and that went like wildfire. So we passed right into the dawn, when the grey came stealing in through the narrow windows and the open door, and making the guttering candles look dissolute; when the men were nodding their heads, and the girls were, many of them, fast asleep in their arms with their heads on the frieze-clad shoulders, and their ruddy lips open in sleep. Well, anyhow, I was

---

46 'diverting to look at'.

47 Performed in 'singing pubs' to this day, but it was dangerous to do so at the turn of the 20th century, when the 'polis' were the tools of the still controlling British Government. This Moriarty is probably unconnected with the villainous Professor in *Sherlock Holmes*, though Conan Doyle, of Irish descent, may conceivably have taken the name from the song.

48 Irish patriotic ballad, written by Joseph Sheridan Le Fanu in 1840. In Stoker's time 'parlour' recitation was popular with private gatherings. Sir Henry Irving was well known for his dramatic recitations, such as that of Thomas Hood's *The Dream of Eugene Aram* in Dublin, which Stoker records as marking his first meeting with the actor. Irving's performance left Stoker close to hysterics.

mighty tired when I came away to drive into Fenagh in the donkey cart and the straw, but felt the effort was not wasted when the whole band of friends – they were real friends now – came down the boreen to see me off, and the poor widow looked gratefully at me as she waved her hand from the open door with the first red of the coming dawn falling full upon her with a sort of promise of hope.'

When the applause had subsided, the Manager stood up and said:

'Ladies and gentlemen, before we go any further I want to see one thing done – to see two very good friends of mine shake hands. Two very good fellows; two leaders and representatives of the great branches of the art that we all love, and whose exercise is our vocation, Tragedy and Comedy. Not that I know such a thing is necessary, for in the close companionship which our work necessitates we can chaff one another without mercy. But there are some strangers here, these gentlemen' – here he pointed to the railway men – 'who are our guests; and I should not like them to think that the girding at each other with passages of humour and satire which has been going on between the accomplished representatives of the buskin and the sock[49] was other than in perfect good fellowship.'

Both men saw the necessity of the case, and each standing up held out a hand.

'Gags, old boy, here's your good health and your family's, and may they live long and prosper,' said the Tragedian.

'Bones, my old pal,' said the Low Comedian, 'here's a nail in your coffin and no hair on your head; and when I regard those hyacinthine locks of yours and see the strength and symmetry of the form of which all your comrades are so proud, I think that is tantamount to the farthest-off manifestation of ill[50] that I can imagine.' The men, who were really old and tried friends, though they had eternal passages of arms, shook hands cordially. The MC

49 'buskin': the high boot of the Tragic Actor. 'sock': ancient soft shoe of the Comic Actor.

50 It is a theatrical superstition to wish ill rather than good, in order to confuse lurking evil spirits. For example, a 'nail in your coffin'. A common well-wishing on an opening night first entrance is 'Break a leg!'

grasped the fact that the situation was complete.

'Next!' he said, indicating the Prompter[51] with the hand which did not contain the hot grog. So the Prompter began:

'I suppose I must confine myself to some personal experience, and that connected with the theatre. It is a pity I am so limited; as if I were free to speak of the adventures of my youth by flood and field, "I could a tale unfold" that would "freeze your young blood and make each particular hair to stand on end like quills upon the fretful porcupine."'

'Talking about floods, what was that about a flood of which you were speaking to Gags the other night? It seemed mighty interesting to both of you.' This from the Heavy Father.

'Oh, that,' answered the Prompter, with a short laugh. 'That wasn't half bad; but it wasn't what you'd call a story; and though I was there, anything that happened was not strictly personal to me. Mr Hupple was there too. He can tell you more about it than I can, for I only knew about going through the flood and what the conductor said; but he heard the confessions.'

'Never mind about him now,' said the MC. 'We shall come to him presently.'

'Tell us about your part, anyhow.' This suggestion came from the Manager. So the Prompter took it as a command – or as a stage direction, at any rate. Bending low, he said:

'Whatever *you* wish, Mr Benville Nonplusser, must be done.'

---

[51] The Prompter can be either an actor or assistant stage manager. A good Prompter can make or break, as he is responsible for following the book exactly and giving correct 'cue' to an actor who has 'dried' (forgotten his dialogue). The 'prompt' is the right-hand corner (when facing the audience) of the stage. The left is 'OP' (off-prompt). If he is cued well, only the actor will know the prompter has been called upon; if badly, then the whole audience also knows, which can be shaming.

6

Mick the Devil

'IT was when I was with the Windsor Theatre Company in America in the 'eighties. I was then Second Lead. Things change, alas![1] Well, we had been North and East and West, and were entering on the last quarter of an eight months' tour when we got to New Orleans.[2] There had been an unusually dry fall,[3] and the rivers were down to the lowest known for years. The earth was all baked and cracked; the trees were burned up with drought, and the grass and undergrowth were as brown as December bracken. The Mississippi[4] was so low that the levees[5] were visible down below the piles, and the water that went swirling by looked as thick as pea-soup. We were playing a three weeks' engagement, before, during, and after Mardi Gras; and as we had been doing two months of one-night stands, we were all glad to have the spell of rest in one place. No one can imagine, till they try it, what a wearisome business it is changing camps every day or every few days. Sometimes you get so dazed with it all that when you wake up in the morning you can't remember where you are – even though you had not been up with the boys the night before.

'Just before Mardi Gras the weather changed. There came for two days a close, damp heat, which was the most terrible thing I ever experienced. It was impossible to keep dry, and I was in nightly fear that the whole paint[6] would wash away from everyone. It was

---

1 The prompter admits having fallen on hard times. He is now employed to prompt other actors, and is presumably reduced to small acting roles.

2 Principal city of Louisiana visited by Stoker during his Irving tours. It is now famous for its jazz as well as Mardi Gras.

3 'fall', known to the British as 'autumn'.

4 One of the world's longest navigable rivers, 2,350 miles long, immortalised by Mark Twain. Edna Ferber's *Showboat* tells the story of one of the floating theatres operating on it.

5 Artificial clay banks designed to protect against rising floods.

6 Theatrical makeup came in sticks of coloured greasepaint (often from Leichner of Germany) blended, then powdered down. Moustaches and beards were stuck on with

just a miracle how moustaches stuck on; and as for the flush of youth and beauty on the girls' cheeks! – well, "there is a Providence that shapes our ends, rough hew them how we will." Then the rain came down. Great Scott! what rain, both as regards quality and quantity! It seemed as if the sky was full of angels emptying buckets. The ground was so hard that at first the rain didn't sink into it, but ran off into the streams and the river. You know what a place New Orleans is! It has its head just above water, when the level is low; but when the Mississippi rises, the levees fill up and the river rushes on high over the city level. We didn't mind the rain, though it spoiled the show in the streets,[7] for it cooled the air, and that was much.

'I certainly never saw anything uglier than the streets of New Orleans. Theoretically, the place is delightful, and if I were only to give you bare facts I should mislead you altogether. What would you think, for instance, of streets by each side of which run streams of water whose gurgling is always in your ears as you walk? Sounds nice, don't it? But then the whole place is clay, and the water is muddy with it; the streams in the streets are full of dirty water, with refuse of all kinds tumbling lazily along. If you dig a foot deep in any street you find water; that is why the gas-pipes are in the air, and why the dead are buried above ground in stucco-covered vaults like bakers' ovens. Well, the rain kept on, and the Mississippi rose till it was up to the top of the levees, and we in New Orleans began to wonder when the city would be flooded out. One day, when I saw the base of the banks beginning to cave in, I felt glad that we were leaving the neighbourhood that night. We were bound for Memphis,[8] and our train was scheduled to leave at one o'clock in the morning. Before turning in, I met the Sectional Engineer tramping up and down and chewing the end of his cigar in a frightful fashion, and we got into conversation. I saw he was anxious, and asked him the cause. He told me in confidence – "in my clothes,"

---

spirit gum. All were subject to the heat from gas stage lighting, and the weather. Humidity would be a threat as colours run and whiskers come loose.

7 Excerpts from plays, rendered in costume, were performed in the streets as an incentive to attract audiences for full performances in the evenings.

8 Memphis was the first stop over the border on the river in Tennessee, crossing through Mississippi County following the river northwards.

he called it – that there had been a "wash-out"[9] in the Valley section of the line, on which it had been arranged that we should travel; and so we would have to go round another way. As I was going on the journey, I was naturally anxious, too, and began to pump him, pretending that I was not at all afraid. He tumbled to it, and explained the trouble to me:

'"You see, I am afraid of Bayou Pierre.[10] There's a spongy gap a couple of miles wide, with a trestle bridge across it over which you have to pass. At the best of times I am anxious about that trestle, for the ground is so bad that anything might happen at any time. But now, with a fortnight's rain and the Mississippi up the levees and the bottoms flooded all over the country, that blessed place will be like an estuary of the sea. The bridge isn't built for weather like this, and the flood is sure to be well over it. A train running on it will have to take chance whether it is there at all; and if any of it is gone – swept away or caved in – well, God help the train! That's all I can say, for everyone in it will die like a rat in a trap!"

'This was distinctly comforting to one of the travellers! I did not know exactly what to do or say, so I just managed to gasp out a question without giving myself away:

'"How long will it take us to get to Bayou Pierre?"

'"Well, say that you start about three o'clock, you will be there about noon or a little before it!" I said good-night and went into the train, determined to wake up pretty early and be ready to have some business in some local town about ten.

I didn't sleep very well, and the grey dawn was edging its way under the dark blind of my sleeping berth when I dropped off. I had plenty of disturbing dreams. The last I remember was that a great crocodile came out of a raging flood, snapped me up in its mouth, and began whirling me along at an inconceivably rapid rate. For a while I tried to make up my mind what I would do. There was no denying the pace at which we were going; I could distinctly hear the whirring of the wheels.

'Then, with a gasp, I remembered that crocodiles don't use

---

9 The levees have collapsed. The ground is now flooded.

10 The map shows a 'Frenchman's Bayou' just north-east of Memphis. Allowing for re-routing as mentioned by the Sectional Engineer, this may be the place.

wheels, and I jumped out of my berth faster even than I usually did when the nigger[11] porter put his black hand over my face or pulled my toes. We seemed to be going at a terrific pace. The carriage rocked to and fro, and I had to hold on, or I should have been thrown about as in a cabin at sea in a storm. I looked out of the window and saw palm and cypress and great swathes of hanging Florida moss[12] on the live-oaks as we whirled by. It was evident we were not going to stop soon. I looked at my watch; it was close to eleven o'clock. I ran back and hammered at the door of the drawing-room of the car where our manager made himself comfortable. He called out "Come in"; I evidently astonished him when I burst in in my pyjamas and a violent state of excitement. "Well, Mr Gallimant, what is it?" he asked shortly, as he stood up. "Do you know," I said, "that we are going to cross a flooded creek on a trestle bridge under water, and that it may be washed away?"

'"No," he said, quite coolly, "I don't! Who has been filling you up with fool-talk?"

'"The engineer of the line told me last night," I answered, unthinkingly.

'"Told you last night!" he said sarcastically. "Then why did you not let me know before? Oh, I see; you wanted to get off in time yourself and let the rest of us meet the danger. You needn't deny it; I see it in your face. Then let me tell you that if you had got off and stayed behind, you'd have found your berth full when you caught us up. See?" I saw pretty well that there was no sympathy to be had from him, so I ran through the train looking for the conductor, whom I found in the observation-room[13] on the last car. Several of the Company, seeing my excitement, took it for granted that something was wrong, and followed me. When we burst in on the conductor, who was making an entry in his book, he looked up and said:

'"Well, what's wrong with you all?"

'"Here, you, stop the train!" I cried. "We want to get out before

---

[11] In common use at the time, the term 'nigger' is nowadays considered racially offensive.

[12] Parasite form of hanging moss common to the half-swamp bayous.

[13] The observation-room has a small open platform at the rear for looking back down the track. US Presidents could also 'meet the people' there.

we're drowned!"

'"Oh, indeed!" he said coolly. "And how do you know you're going to be drowned?"

'"Because," I said, in a heat, "we are going to run over Bayou Pierre on the trestle bridge, and it's under water. Who knows that part of it mayn't be washed away or have collapsed?" He actually smiled at me.

'"Now, do you know," he said, "that shows great knowledge, both topographical and problematical, on your part! And so you want to get out? Well, you can't. Tell you why? Mick Devlin was put on to drive this train because he's the daringest driver on the whole fit-out. 'Mick the Devil' they call him. And Mick is letting her go now for all she is worth. Listen to that; she's going seventy, clean.[14] Mick knows his part of the job, and I guess you've all got to keep your hair on and sit tight while Mick has his hand on the throttle."'

'Here's luck to Mick!' said the driver of the engine, in a hearty voice.

'Hush, h-s-s-h!' said the rest, for they were getting interested in the story. The Prompter went on:

'"Why does he want to go so fast?" I said.

'"Now you're beginning to talk!" he answered; "and as you know so much, I'll tell you more. Mick knows what he's about; what he doesn't know about engines and bridges and floods isn't much worth knowin'. See? We've got to go across Bayou Pierre to-day; and belike we'll be the last to cross it before the floods go down. You know some of the dangers, but you don't know as much as Mick. Someone has been fillin' you up with bogey talk, and you've taken it not only for Gospel, but for all the Gospel there is. The Sectional Engineer is a permanent-way man, and he looks on his work from the standpoint of statical force.[15] But, you see, Mick's special province is dynamics. He knows all the dangers that there Engineer ladled into you; and he takes his chances on them blindfold, for he can do nothing. If there is a wash-out or a collapse anywhere, it's

---

14 The train's speed was seventy miles per hour.

15 The physics concerned with bodies at rest, in equilibrium. Dynamics is the treatment of motion itself.

kingdom-come for us all, anyhow. But then there's other dangers that Mick knows, and I know; mayhap the Sectional Engineer knows them, too, though he didn't talk of them, for they don't belong to his trade."[16]

'"What are the other dangers?" I gasped out with what appearance of nonchalance I could muster, for the doorway was crowded with a lot of deadly-white faces. The conductor actually smiled as he replied:

'"I guess I'd better explain" – here he actually laughed – "though I daresay some of ye think it's pretty tiresome listening to a dissertation on coming dangers whilst a mad Irishman is whirling you all to perdition. Well, be it so! Your own boss made a contract. The railway company agreed to it; and Mick and me undertook to carry it out. Our Yard-Master said we was to put you down in Nashville,[17] flood or no flood; and so we shall, the will of God alone objectin'. An' what the will of God is we'll try to find out for sure. You see, this flood has been out nigh on a week. Floods in a big place like Bayou Pierre don't, as a rule, run strong enough to wash clean away like a sea or a big river does. But it can weaken. It eddies everlastingly round the bases of piles, and it softens the mortar between the bricks of the piers. There's a lot of them in this bridge we're coming to, for though you'll hardly believe it when you see it, it's only a flat valley, except in floods, with streams running through it here and there. When pierwork or brickwork is demoralised and weakened that way, though it will stand all right till it gets a shock, it will suddenly go all to bits if it gets jarred. You know what that means. Each pier holds a piece of a bridge; and if it goes, down goes the whole thing. Now, have any of you ever thought of the weight, the deadweight, of a train? Such a one as ours will weigh, engine and tender and brake and goods and passengers and all, more than half a million pounds. Put that suddenly on the top of one of these tottering piles or weakened piers, and what'll happen? Why, the darned thing will slide, or warp, or twist, or crumble away, or grind together; and this, mind you, without a steady force of water to

---

16 Typical 'union' thinking. Never intrude in another man's 'trade' area.

17 We now learn the train's destination is Nashville, some 200 miles east of Memphis, so the 'Frenchman's Bayou' becomes more probable.

wash away every fragment of mortar as it is disturbed. So as we travel over them we're helping to make the wash-outs and collapses that the Sectional Engineer fears."

'He paused, and through the beating of my own heart and the throbbing of the pulses in my own head I could hear a sort of sobbing groan from the womenkind – they were far too frightened to scream. Without was the whirring rush of the wheels and the panting of the engine taxed to its utmost with our terrific speed. The Conductor looked keenly into the faces of all before he went on:

'"Now, Mick knows all about this, and he also knows the way to minimise the risk. Why, he's doin' it now; that is why he's goin' at our present pace! Mick's workin' this job bald-headed!"[18]

'"Why?" The question was gasped out by one of the ladies, her eyes as round as a bird's with fright. The Conductor nodded approval.

'"Now, that's good! I like to see people that's reasonable and don't quite let their fears master them. Well, ma'am, I'll tell you why. A pier can't fall all in a second; it takes time to break up anything that it has taken time to put together, even if it has to be hoisted with dynamite. Now, our pressure is great, but it doesn't last long. The quicker we go, the shorter it lasts; so that when things are real bad – so near a collapse that it only wants a finishing touch – we can be up and over before the crash comes. I've seen Mick take a train through three feet of water in a flood on one of the Pan Handle[19] branches, and felt the last car pull up the slope of the girders of a bridge as the pier collapsed behind us. Don't you be skeered,[20] any of you! Mick's the right man in the right place; an' if you're goin' to get through to-day he's the man to take you. If not, we're well out of it compared with him! Drownin' is an easy death, they say; but if the engine goes down head first, as she will if there be aught[21] wrong, there's steam enough in the boilers and heat enough to cook him and his mate while they're drownin'!

---

18 Without pausing to put on one's hat, in other words 'with great haste'.

19 Several US states, among them Texas, Oklahoma and Florida, are shaped with a slab of land (the panhandle) that appears stuck onto the rest.

20 'skeered': scared.

21 'aught': anything.

'"Well, s'long! I'm goin' up to the baggage-car in front to be near Mick. We've worked together too long to be parted at the last, if it should come. There she goes! we're into Bayou Pierre now, and so long as we're on the trestle, all any of you can do is to say your prayers and confess your sins. After that – well, I don't think I'd worry much about it as yet!"

'He passed on his way, leaving behind him a sense of gallant manhood[22] that made me ashamed of being afraid.

'The speed had manifestly diminished, although we still went at a considerable rate; there was a queer sound, a sort of hissing scream as the water was churned by our rushing wheels.

'I stepped out on the rear platform and looked around. In front of me, as I stood, the shore we had left receded farther and farther at every instant. The dwarf palms became a stunted mass, and the clumps of cypress and live-oak seemed to dwindle away into shrubs. Around us was a waste of water flowing swiftly under our feet; a great frothy yellow tide, with here and there floating masses of *débris* – logs, hay, dead cattle, and drift of every imaginable kind. On either side it was the same. Leaning out over the rail I could just see the far shore, a dim line on the horizon. We were driving through the flood at a great pace and our engine sent before us, as does the prow of a steamer, a wave whose flanks fell ever back on us as we swept along. Now and again we could feel a sort of shiver or a sudden shock, as though something had loosened or given way under us. But somehow we ran along all right; and as the shore we had passed grew dimmer, and as the far shore grew closer, our spirits rose and the fear fell away from us.

'It was with glad hearts that we felt the solid ground under us and heard the old roar of the wheels again. The squealing of the brakes was like music as we drew up on the track a little later on.

'The engine seemed to pant like an animal which has gone through hard stress; and her master, Mick the Devil, looking gay[23] and easy and debonnair, raised his cap in answering salute as we all

---

[22] The first essential quality demanded by Stoker of any heroic male. He uses the words 'gallant manhood', or similar, to describe male characters in *Dracula* and throughout his fiction.

[23] 'gay' originally meant 'exuberant and full of life', without reference to sexual orientation.

tumbled out and raised three cheers for him in true Anglo-Saxon fashion.'

'Now, Mr Hupple,' said the MC, 'as we learned from Gallimant that you were on the train crossing Bayou Pierre, and that you heard the confessions, perhaps you will tell us something of what happened?' There came a chorus of entreaty from all, amongst which the voices of the ladies were the most eager. Confessions – of other people – are always interesting. The Second Low Comedian[24] had a hint of the duty before him, and seemed quite prepared. He began at once:

---

[24] Low Comics work as a double act, one having the other to 'knock down' and to act as the 'foil' to number one.

7
In Fear of Death

'OUR little lot comprised the major part of the Company. None of them had talked to the Sectional Engineer, and so were not prepared to save their own skins by bolting without ever giving a hint to their pals. I never knew the full measure of our friend's bravery before!'

'Time!' said the MC, warningly. He nodded cheerfully and went on:

'It was only when we were actually in the water that any of them began to concern themselves. Indeed, at first no one seemed to mind, for we had often before made a dash over a flooded stream. But when the speed slackened and the rush of the wheels in the water made a new sort of sound, they all ran to the windows and looked out. Some of the festive spirits thought it a good opportunity to frighten the girls, and put up a joke on the more timid of the men. It didn't seem a difficult job so far as some of them were concerned, for the surprise was rapidly becoming terror. Everything seemed to lend itself to the presiding influence; the yellow water seeming to go two ways at once as it flowed past us and as we crossed its course; the horrible churning of our wheels which seemed to come up from under us through the now opened windows; the snorting and panting of the engine; the looks of fear and horror growing on the blanching faces around; all seemed to culminate towards hysteria. The most larky of the men was young Gatacre, who was understudy for Huntley Vavasseur, then our Leading Juvenile. He pretended to be terribly afraid, and cowered down and hid his face and groaned, all the time winking at some of us. But presently, as the waste of water grew wider and wider, his glances out of the window became more anxious, and I could see his lips grow white. All at once he became ghastly pale, and, throwing up his hands, broke out into a positive wail of terror, and began to pray in a most grovelling manner – there is no other way to describe it. To some of us it was revolting, and we should have liked to kick him; but its effect on the girls was dreadful. All the hysteria of panic which had been coming on broke out at once, and within half a minute the place was like the Stool-of-Repentance corner at a Revival Meeting.[1]

'I am glad to say that, with these exceptions, they were in the main brave and sensible people, who kept their own heads and tried to make, for very shame's sake, their friends keep theirs. It seems to me that really good women are never finer than when they are helping a weak sister. I mean really helping when it isn't altogether pleasant work. I don't count it help to a woman, lashing out wastefully with other people's Eau de Cologne, and ostentatiously loosening her stays,[2] and then turning to the menkind who are looking on helplessly, with a "phew!" as if they knew what was wrong with her all the time. We all know how *our* women help each other, for we are all comrades, and the girls are the best of us. But on this occasion the womenkind were a bit panicky, and even those who kept their heads and tried to shield the others from the effects of their hysterical abandon, were pale and rocky themselves, and kept one eye on the yellow flood running away under us.

'I certainly never did hear such a giving away as in the confessions of some of them, and I tell you that it wasn't pleasant to listen to. It made some of us men angry and humiliated to think that we could be so helpless. We took some of the girls and tried to actually shake them back into reason, but, Lord bless you! it wasn't the least use. The more we shook them, the more we shook out of them things which were better left unsaid. It almost seemed as if confession was a pebbly sort of thing that could be jerked out of one, like corn out of a nose-bag.[3] The whole thing was so infernally sudden that one had no time to think. One moment we were all composed and jolly, and the next there were these poor women babbling out

---

1 These are still in use in some Welsh chapels. The 'Stool' was where the sinner stood or sat and confessed all.

2 'stays'. The restricting whalebone corset was in common use at the turn of the 20th century and remained the principal shaper of the female form until World War I, by which time they were laced up over hooks at the front.

3 The canvas bag placed over a horse's head, full of dry feed.

the most distressing and heartrending things, and we quite unable to stop them. The funny thing, as it seemed to me now, was that it never occurred to any of us to shove off and leave them alone! Anyhow, we didn't go, at all events till the fat was in the fire. Fortunately, the poor girls didn't have much to confess that seemed very wrong to most of us. There were one or two nasty and painful things, of course, but we all shut our memories, and from that day to this it never made any difference in any way that I could ever see – except in one case, where a wife told an old story to her husband. I can see the scene now. The terror in her grey eyes, the frown in his pale face, all the whiter by contrast with his hair. "Sun and Shade," we used to call them.'

He broke off suddenly, paused a moment, and then resumed:

'But that was their own business, and though it never seemed to come right, none of us ever said a word about it.'

'Did none of the men confess anything?' asked the Singing Chambermaid. There was in the tone of her voice that underlying note of militant defiance which is always evident when the subject of woman in the abstract is mentioned in mixed company. The Second Low Comedian smiled as he replied:

'Certainly, my dear! I thought you understood that I was speaking of the young ladies of both sexes. You remember that the first, in fact the one to set them off, was an alleged Man.'[4]

'Well, these things, you see, made the painful side of the incident, for it is not pleasant to hear people say things which you know they will grieve for bitterly afterwards. But there was another side, which was both interesting and amusing: the way in which the varieties of character came out in the confessions, and the manner of their coming. If we hadn't known already – I speak for myself – we should have been able to differentiate the weaknesses of the various parties, and to have got a knowledge of the class of things which they fondly hoped they had kept hidden. I suppose it is such

---

[4] Stoker had definite views on the behaviour of his men and women, 'manliness' being the first priority of the male. His male fictional heroes appear to be mainly based on his own personality, as he wished it.

times that reveal us to ourselves, or would do so if we had grace to avail ourselves of our opportunities. Anyhow, the dominant note of each personality was struck in so marked a way that the scene became a sort of character-garden with living flowers!'

When the applause which followed his poetic 'tag' had ceased, there was a chorus of indignant disappointment:

'Is that all?'

'Why stop just as it was getting interesting?'

'Just fancy, with material like that, to fade out in vague generalities!'

'Can't you tell us some more of the things they said?'

'What's the use of telling us of confessions when you keep it dark what they were.'

'Was there anything so very compromising, to you or to anybody else, that you should hesitate?'

'That's just it,' said the Second Low Comedian with a grin. 'If there was anything compromising, I would tell it with pleasure, especially, I need not say, if it concerned myself. But of all the confessions that were ever written or spoken, I suppose there never were any as little compromising as on this occasion. With the one exception that I have spoken of, and on which all our lips are sealed, there was nothing which would injure the character of a sergeant in the Archangelic[5] police force. Of course, I except the young man who began the racket. There was not one of those who "confessed" who did not compromise himself or herself. But the subjects were so odd! I didn't know there were so many sinless wickednesses in the whole range of evil!'

'What on earth do you mean?' said the Leading Lady with the wide open eyes of stage amazement. 'Do give us some examples, so that we may be able to follow you.'

'Ah! I thought that was what you wanted!' he answered with a wink. 'You would like to hear the confessions, good or bad, or, rather, bad or worse, and judge for yourself as to their barometric wickedness. All right! I will tell you all I remember.

'There was our Leading Lady, I mention no names, who had

---

5 If the Archangel Gabriel headed a police force it was morally safe.

been on the stage, to my own knowledge, twenty-eight years, and she was in the Second Lead when I met her first at Halifax[6] in *Wibster's Folly*, which was a popular stock piece on the Yorkshire Circuit.[7] She confessed to having deceived, not only the public, but her friends, even her dear friends of the Company, and would like to put herself right with them all and have their forgiveness ere she died. Her sin was one of vanity, for she had deceived them as to her age. She had acknowledged to twenty-nine; but now in her last hour, with the death drops on her brow, and the chill of the raging flood already striking into her very soul, she would confess. They knew how hard it was for a woman to be true when dealing with her age; women at least would understand her; she would confess that she was really thirty-three.[8] Then she sank down on her knees, in a picturesque position, which she had often told her friends she made famous in *East Lynne*,[9] and held up her hands and implored their forgiveness. Do you know that nearly all those present were so touched by her extraordinary self-sacrifice in that trying moment, that they turned away and hid their faces in their hands. I could myself see the shoulders of some of them shake with emotion.

'Well, her example was infectious; she was hardly on her knees when our Juvenile Lead took up the running. With a heart-breaking bitter sob, such as adorned his performance in *Azrael the Prodigal*, he held his hands aloft with the fingers interlaced, and, looking up to the gallery[10] – I mean the roof, or the sky, or whatever he saw above him with either his outer or his inner eye – he mourned his malingering in the way of pride. He had been filled with ungodly pride,

---

6 The nearby towns of Halifax and Huddersfield were usually twinned dates on the Yorkshire circuit.

7 As Yorkshire was the largest county in England, a company could fix so many dates within it that it formed a 'circuit' of its own. Audiences in Yorkshire were, and are, reputed to be 'slower' than in the South, though nevertheless deeply appreciative and loyal.

8 Readers can doubtless think of many actresses of which the same can be said to apply.

9 Popular drama by Mrs Henry Wood at the turn of the 20th century. It continued into the middle of the century as 'melodrama', with deliberate over-emphasis (ham acting). *East Lynne* was a consistent success in repertory.

10 The term 'playing to the gallery' is still in wide use today. It stems from the actors' habit of directing their performance to the cheap seats up high, where the audience was the most enthusiastic.

when during his very first engagement, having been promoted through sheer merit – having swept, if he might say so, upward like a rocket through the minor ranks of the profession, he had emerged in sober splendour amongst the loftier altitudes. Oh, even that fact had not bounded his excesses of pride. That evil quality, which, like jealousy,[11] "mocks the meat it feeds on," had grown with the enlarging successes which seemed to whirl upon him like giant snowflakes from the Empyrean.[12] When the *Mid-Mudland Anti-Baptist Scrutiniser* had spoken of him as "the rising histrionic genius who was destined to lift from the shrouded face of Melpomene[13] the seemingly ineradicable shadow which the artistic incompetence of a re-puritanised age had thrown upon it," he had felt elated with the thought that on his shoulder rested the weight of the banner of art, which it would be his duty, as well as his pride, to carry amongst the Nations, and unfurl even before the eyes of their Kings. Ah! but that was not his worst sin, for with the years that had carried the greatness of his stormy youth into the splendour of his prime young manhood, had grown an ever-increasing pride in what he knew from the adoring looks of women and their passionate expressions of endearment – both written and verbal – was the divine gift of physical beauty in perfection. In which gift was included the voice at once sweet and powerful which evoked that enthusiastic tribute from the *Bootle Local Government Questioner*, wherein occurred the remarkable passage: "It is rare, if not unique, to find in the tones of a human voice, centred in no matter how perfect a physical *entourage*, at once the subtlety of the lyre, the great epigrammatic precision of the ophicleide,[14] and the resonant doom-sounding thunder of the clarion and the bassoon." So, too, was included a bearing of grace and nobility which "recalled" as the Midland humoristic organ, *The Pushful Joe*, remarked, "the worth of the youthful

---

11 Pride and Jealousy are two of the 'seven deadly sins'.

12 The highest part of Heaven, containing the pure elements of fire, water and air. Thought by early Christians to be the abode of God. The theatrical term for the gallery is 'the gods'.

13 Melpomene is the Muse of Tragedy. The Second Low Comedian is 'classically' inclined.

14 A keyed brass wind instrument, or a powerful organ reed pipe.

emperor Gluteus Maximus."[15] Oh! these things were indeed sources of a pride, which was at best a weakness of poor humanity. Still, it should be held in check, and this in proportion to its natural strength. "Mea culpa! Mea culpa!"[16] he said in the tones with which he used to thrill the house in *Don Alzavar the Penitent, or the Monk of Madrid.* He went on further, for pride seemed to have no limit, but essayed, when fixed in daring and lofty natures, to scale the very bastions of Olympus.[17] He was proud – oh, so proud that in this dread moment, when he stood hand-in-hand with his fellow-brother, Death, he could see its earthly littleness. It was when depicting the *rôles* in which he had won his greatest fame, he had, with the best and purest intention, he assured us, dared the blue ribbon of histrionic achievement in essaying the part of *Hamlet* in the Ladbroke Hall.[18] He had found his justification of Metropolitan endeavour in the striking words of the *Westbourne Grove and Neighbouring Parishes' Chronicle of Striking Events*: "The triumph of our youngest 'Hamlet' is as marked as his many successes in less ambitious walks of histrionic renown!"'

He was interrupted by our First Low Comedy Merchant, who said:

'Time! old man. There are others who want a chance of public confession whilst Death still stares us in the face.' He was followed by our Heavy Man, who added:

'It's a good idea, as well as a new one, to confess your Notices.[19] Anyhow, it makes a variety from having to pretend to read them every time you strike a man for a drink.' The Leading Juvenile glared at his interrupters, in the manner which he was used to

---

15 The Gluteus Maximus is the large muscle of the human buttock. From 'gloutos': rump.

16 'I am to blame!'

17 The legendary home of the Gods of Ancient Greece. The real mountain is in Thessaly in modern Greece.

18 Notting Hill in west London was at the turn of the 20th century teeming with small theatres and halls, many of which were hired by enthusiastic performers anxious to display their accomplishments. The Ladbroke was one of these. The term 'essaying' suggests either a play reading rather than a full costume performance, or a posh synonym for 'attempting'.

19 'Notices': Reviews.

assume as Geoffrey Plantagenet[20] in *The Baffled Usurper*. He was about to loose the vials of his wrath upon them when our First Singing Chambermaid, who had been furtively preparing for her effort by letting down her back hair,[21] flung herself upon her knees with a piercing shriek, and, holding up her hands invocatively after the manner of *The Maiden's Prayer*, cried out, interrupting herself all the while with muttered sobs of choking anguish:

'"Oh, ye Powers, to whom is given the priceless guardianship of Maiden life, look down in forgiving pity upon the delinquencies of one who, though without evil purpose, but in the guilelessness of her innocent youth, and with the surpassing cruelty of the young and thoughtless, hath borne hard upon the passionate but honourable love of Dukes and Marquises! Peccavi! Peccavi!! Peccavi!!!"[22] with which final utterance she fell fainting upon her face, and struggled convulsively, till, seeing that no one flew to her assistance, she lay still a moment, and then ignominiously rose to her feet and retired, outwardly sobbing and inwardly scowling, to her section.

'Hardly, however, had she spoken her tag when two aspirants for confessional honours sought to "catch the speaker's eye." One of them was the Understudy of the last confessor, the other the First Old Woman. They were something of an age and appearance, each being on the shady side of something, and stout in proportion. They both had deep voices, and as neither would at first give way, their confessions were decidedly clamorous and tangled, but full of divine possibilities of remorse. They both had flung themselves on their knees, right and left, like the kneeling figures beside an Elizabethan tomb. We all stood by, with admiring sympathy manifested in our choking inspirations and on our broadening smiles. It was a pretty fair struggle. The First Old Woman was fighting for her position, and that is a strong stimulus to effort; the other was endeavouring to win a new height in her Olympian ambition, and that is also a strong aid to endeavour. They both talked so loud and so fast that none of us could follow a word that either of them said.

---

20 Father of Henry II (of Thomas à Becket fame) and first of the Plantagenet Kings (1154-1189).

21 The Singing Maid lets down her coiffure to physically declare her abandonment! She gives a 'spontaneous' audition beyond her normal parts.

22 Latin for 'I have sinned'. This is a highly 'literate' company.

But neither would give way, till our Tragedian, beginning to despair of an opening for his confession, drew a deep breath and let us have it after the manner of his celebrated impersonation of the title-*rôle* of *Manfred*[23] in the Alpine storm, in which you will remember that he has to speak against the thunder, the bassoon, the wind, and the rain - not to mention the avalanches, though he generally makes a break for them to pass. The women held out as long as they could, and finally, feeling worsted by the Tragedian's thunder, they joined against the common enemy, and shrieked hysterically in unison as long as their breath held out. Our Tragedian's confession was immense. I wish I could remember it word for word as he gave it, with long dwelling on his pet words, and crashing out his own particular consonants. We were all silent, for we wanted to remember, for after use, what he said. Being a Tragedian, he began, of course, with Jove:

'"Thou Mighty One who sittest on the cloud-capped heights of Olympus,[24] and regardest the spectral figure of the mighty Hyster seated in his shadowy cart, deign to hear the murmurings of a heart whose mightiest utterances have embodied the noblest language of the chiefest bards. Listen, O son of Saturn! O husband of Juno! O father of Thalia and Melpomene! O brother of Neptune and Pluto! O lover of Leda and Semele and Danae and of all the galaxy of celestial beauties who crowned with love the many-sided proclivities of Thou, most multitudinous-hearted God! Hear the sad wail of one who has devoted himself to the Art of Roscius![25] Listen to the voice that has been wont to speak in thundrous tones to the ears of a wondering world, now stilled to the plaintive utterance of deepening regret. Hear me mourn the lost opportunities of a not-unsuccessful life! When I think that I have had at my foot the ball of

---

[23] The poetic dramas of Lord Byron were performed throughout the 19th century. Interestingly, Byron was the first to transfer the vampire image from peasant to doomed immortal of poetic stature. His 'fragment' was reworked by his physician, Dr John Polidori, as 'The Vampyre' in 1819. Planche's 'The Vampire, or The Bride of the Isles', the following year, marked the introduction on stage of the 'vampire trap', comprising two spring leaves in the backcloth or floor, so arranged that the actor's body appears to pass through a solid wall.

[24] The Tragedian mixes Greek and Roman Mythology, but is, after all, only interested in the sound, not the literal meaning, of his words.

[25] Quintus Roscius Gallus. 62BC. Famous Roman actor.

success, and in my sublime indifference spurned it from me as a thing of little worth, well knowing that in all the years genius such as mine must ever command the plaudits of an enraptured world, what can I say or how announce the magnitude, or even the name, of my sin? Hear me then, O mighty Jove ..."

'Just then the dull threshing and swishing of the submerged wheels changed to the normal roar and resonance, as we left the trestle bridge and swept into the cutting beyond. The first one to speak was the Prompter, who said:

'"Your attack was a little slow, Mr Montressor. It's a bit hard that the curtain has to drop before the invocation is properly begun!"

There was a pause, chiefly utilised for the consumption of heeltaps and the replenishment of drinking vessels. It was broken by the voice of one of the Young Men who sat at some distance from the fire and quite away from the Prompter – a Young Man who wore his hair long and had literary ambitions. He spoke of himself sometimes as 'a Man of Letters as well as a Player.'

'How small the world is! Do you know that out of that very episode that Mr Hupple has just spoken of came a strange circumstance? If I were next on the list I could give it as a fitting corollary.'

'Corolly or no corolly,' the Sewing Woman was heard to murmur, the punch having had some effect in creating a certain drowsiness which fell on her like a robe. 'Corolly or no corolly, it ain't in it with the Dead Byby I was a-tellin' ye of.'

The MC stopped the threatened reminiscence by shaking her by the shoulder. 'Wake up, dear lady,' he said, 'and learn of the smallness of the world. I think we may take it,' he added, looking round, 'that in such an exceptional case we may break the rule and ask Bloze to go on next.' 'Bloze' was the nickname of Mr Horatio Sparbrook (stage name) given to him for an attempt he had once made to introduce realism into the part of Gaspard in *The Lady of Lyons*[26] in replying to Claude's entreaty to pardon the blows which he had

---

[26] Edward Bulwer Lytton's 1838 play was revived in 1879 by Henry Irving at the Lyceum, where Gaspard (sic) was played by Frank Tyars. The character's correct name is Gaspar.

received in his service: 'Bloze! Melnotte, Bloze! Bloze!' instead of the traditional 'Balows! Melnotte, Balows! Balows!' Without further preface Mr Sparbrook began:

'Mr Hupple mentioned that in that memorable journey across the flooded Bayou Pierre a certain confession was made. May I ask if that was done in your hearing?' Considerable curiosity was manifested, and the faces of all were turned towards the Second Low Comedian, awaiting his reply. After a pause it came with a certain reluctance:

'Yes, more than one of us did hear the confession. No one seemed to mind it at the time; but there was a painful result. There were few words, but they meant much. We didn't ever see them speaking to each other after that, but when that tour ended they both resigned, and I never saw either of them again. Someone told me that they had both given up the stage! I'd like to know how you came to know of it. There was a sort of understanding amongst those of us who saw the scene and heard what was said that we wouldn't ever speak of it. I've never done so from that time to this.'

'Was he a tall, well-featured man, with clustering grey hair?'

'It was black then; as black as Bones's! I beg your pardon, old man' – this to the Tragedian. The Young Man continued:

'And was she handsome and somewhat aquiline?[27] A fine woman with a presence, and thick white hair, and grey eyes like stars?'

'She had beautiful grey eyes as big and bright as lamps, but her hair was golden. They were the handsomest young couple I think I ever saw; and up to that time I believe they simply doted on each other. I tell you it was a grief to us all what happened that journey.' The Young Man said very gravely:

'If we knew everything, as the Almighty knows it, perhaps we should regret some things more than we do, and others less. I only guessed that Bayou Pierre was the scene of that confession; the other end of the story comes from across the world.' There was a shiver of expectation from all. Here was a good story that seemed to have a living interest. A stillness, as marked as that of the falling snow without, reigned in the car.

---

[27] Eagle-featured, from 'aquila': eagle. More bluntly, with a hooked or Roman nose.

8

At last

'WHEN I was young – I'm not very old yet, but I was very young then, and it all seems long ago – I made an ass of myself. It wasn't very bad, not criminal; but I was pretty well ashamed of it, for my people were of high rank and held a great position in the county. When I came back I was afraid to tell the girl I was engaged to. She was a clever girl, and she knew by a sort of instinct that there was *something*, and asked me what it was. I denied that there was anything. That did for me, for I knew she was clean grit,[1] and that she would have the truth or nothing, and as I didn't want to tell her I was a liar as well as an ass, I shoved[2] for Australia. What I did there doesn't concern you much, and it was pretty tame, anyhow. I only mention this that you may understand something later. I had been a medical student, and liked the work so well that I have had a sneaking fondness for everything connected with it ever since. On the ship I went out on was a nurse, who was going out as an assistant matron to one of the Melbourne hospitals. She was a young woman, but with white hair; and she used to come down to the steerage[3] – where I was – and try to be of service. I had become a kind of volunteer help to the doctor, who recognised that I *had been* a gentleman – you *are* not much of a gentleman in a steerage, I can tell you – and made things a little comfortable for me in several ways. By being about with him I met the nurse, and we became very good friends. She was very sympathetic, and knew pretty well that I was sore-hearted about something; and with the natural sweet helpfulness of a woman – God bless 'em![4] – soon got to know my secret. One night – I shall never forget it, a heavy, still night with the moon a blaze of gold over the

---

1 Obstinate in her virtue.

2 pushed off (the boat); that is, 'took a boat to Australia'.

3 The lowest deck, close to the engines and propeller (screw), providing the cheapest passage for the poorest passengers.

4 Typical gushing Stoker, trembling of lip, hand on heart.

silent sea – we sat out late, right over the screw, which ground away beneath us but disturbed us no more than the ticking of a clock. The mystery of the place, and the hunger for sympathy which always gnawed at my soul, got the better of me, and I opened my heart as I have never done before or since. When I stopped I saw that her great eyes were gleaming out over the sea, and the tears were rolling down her cheeks. She turned to me and took my hand between both of hers and said:

'"Oh! why didn't you tell her all? She would have forgiven all – everything, and would have loved you better for it all your life long. It is the concealment that hurts! Noble natures feel it most. I know, I know it too well, out of the bitterness of my broken heart!" I saw here a sorrow far greater than my own, and tried to comfort her. It seemed a relief to her, as it had been to me, to speak of her trouble, and I encouraged her confidence. She told me that in her youth she had run away with a man whom she thought she loved; they were married at a registry,[5] but after a while she found out that he was married already. She wanted to leave him then at once, but he terrorised her, threatening to kill her if she tried to leave him. So she had perforce to remain with him till, happily, he met with a fatal accident and she was free. Then her baby was born dead, and she found herself alone.'

Here there was an interruption on the part of the Sewing Woman, who remarked *sotto voce*:[6]

'He's a-tykin' of *my* Dead Byby, too!'

'Hush! hush!' said the MC. And the Young Man went on:

'She changed her name, and after trying work of several kinds, found her way on the stage. There she fell in love, in real love, with a man she honoured; and when she found that he loved her too, she was afraid to tell him the dark chapter of her life lest she should lose him. She thought that as it was all past, and as no trace remained, no one need ever know. She was married and was ideally

---

5 Local Registry Office for births, deaths and marriages. It is a legal requirement in Britain to register all three. Couples marry in a Registry Office rather than a Church either by choice (being non-Christian) or necessity (Churches would not always marry those previously divorced).

6 Quietly, in an undertone.

happy, and, after a couple of years, which had brought them a daughter, towards the end of a certain tour was on her way home where she would see her little baby daughter again, when in a time of great peril, when everyone round her was making confession of all they had ever done wrong, she was drawn into the hysterical whirlpool, and told her husband all that had been. He seemed cut to the heart, but said very little – not a word of reproach. Then she, too, felt constrained to silence, and a barrier seemed to grow up between them, so that when they reached England – home was a name only, and not a reality – they did not seem able to speak freely; and it became apparent to both that nothing remained but to separate. He had wished to take the child, and when the subject was mooted, said he wanted to take her far away where she would never know what had been. "Oh, I loved him so," she wailed, "that I felt that all I could give him was my child. The baby when she grew up would never know her mother's shame. It was a bitter atonement for my deceit; but it was all I could do. Perhaps God will account it to me and my child and the husband that I love, and somehow turn it to usefulness in His good time."

'Well, I comforted her as well as I could, though there was not much comfort to her in the world, poor soul, separated from her husband, whom she still loved, and from their child. We became fast friends, and we often wrote to each other; and in all my wanderings I kept her informed of my whereabouts.

'I went up-country herding,[7] and after a weary, weary time on

'The bitter road the younger son must tread
Ere he win to hearth and saddle of his own,[8]
Mid the riot of the shearers[9] in the shed
In the silence of the herder's hut alone,'

I found my way to a lonely place on the edge of a creek.[10] It was a

---

7 Towards the East Mountains or perhaps across the border into New South Wales. All good sheep country.

8 A man who owns his own horse is on the way up. To steal a horse was a capital offence in Australia at this time.

9 Confirmation that he was tending and shearing sheep, and living as a hired hand under rough circumstances.

lovely spot, and the man who owned it had evidently given time and care to its beautifying, for all the natural trees and flowers were used to the best advantage, and it was a delight to see growing with the added luxuriance of a new soil all the home flowers as well. My employer, Mr Macrae, was a crank in some ways, but he was a gentleman, and he made my life a very different one from what it had been in my stock-keeping apprenticeship. He, too, soon recognised that I had been a gentleman, and took me into the house instead of letting me camp outside in a rough shed, as is the usual thing with hired hands. Oh! the comfort and luxury of being in a real house with real bedding and real food, after a bunk and damper[11] of your own making. Mr Macrae was very kindly, but stern on certain points. He simply idolised his little daughter, a bright, pretty child with golden hair and big grey eyes that I seemed, when I saw them, to have known all my life. The sun seemed to the father to rise and set in the child; but even to her he could be stern, even cruel, to an extent I never saw equalled. One night after dinner the little thing was nestling up to him and playing with him in her usual coaxing way. He asked her some little question, and she fenced with the answer. This seemed all at once to make him stern, and he asked some more questions with a fierce gravity which frightened the child. She attempted playfulness as a weapon against wrath, as a woman does; but the father would have none of it. He brushed it aside and continued his inquisition. It was quite apparent to me that the child had little or nothing to conceal, but she was frightened, and in her fear yielded to the weakness of the woman[12] within her and lied. It was a harmless little lie at worst, one rather of not telling the truth than of speaking falsely; but it seemed to inflame the father to a white heat. His eyes glowed with the intensity of his anger. He mastered himself, however, and his cold anger was infinitely worse than his hot. He took the child very tenderly in his arms and said:

---

[10] Creeks are often shallow with a stony bed. They usually dry out in early summer, becoming heavy only after the heavy summer rains.

[11] The stockman carried his own bedding and was provided with basic slatted bunk and 'damper', an upright cast-iron stove for heating and cooking.

[12] Stoker moralises again. The ways of a woman – that is, essentially weak in moral fibre!

'"Little one, you know that I love you?"

'"Yes, daddy!" came the pretty voice, in a flood of tears.

'"And you know I wouldn't hurt you but for your good, darling?"

'"Yes, daddy! But, oh, daddy, daddy, don't hurt me! – don't hurt me!"

'"I must, my little one, I must! You will have to remember all your life what it is to lie; that fire on earth or in hell is the liar's portion. And it is better that you learn it now than suffer it hereafter and make others suffer!" He bent down towards the fire, holding her hand in his; her pitiful little struggles were as nothing in his powerful grasp. Seeing me instinctively draw near, for I thought to protect the child, he motioned me back gravely.

'"Do not interfere. It is necessary that my child learn a little lesson to save her a harder one later on."

'With an iron determination, and with lips set and growing white as snow, he put for a moment the rosy fingers of the child on the hot bar of the grate. Despite her shriek of pain, he held it there quite a second or two, and then drew her back almost fainting. The child loved and trusted him in spite of the cruel act, and clung to him, sobbing as if her little heart would break. He held her close to him, and then disengaged her arm very gently from his neck. He stepped closer to the fire, and saying to her: "See, little one, you have no pain that is not mine!" thrust his own right hand down into the very heart of the glowing fire. He held it there a few seconds without a quiver, whilst the child shrieked and flew to him and dragged the hand away.

'"Oh, daddy, daddy, daddy!" she wailed, "and I have by my lying made you suffer this!" As I am a living man, I saw a glad light flash into his eyes, though the pain he suffered must have been excruciating. With his other hand he stroked the child's golden locks as he said:

'"It was worth pain, my little one, that you should learn so great a truth."

'I could not but be silent in face of such a splendid heroism,[13] and offered to use such medical knowledge as I possessed on his

---

13 Heroism? Some might describe this as Calvanistic Scottish idiocy.

behalf. He accepted cheerfully, and when I had got oil and lint he made me dress the child's burn before allowing me to attend to his own. It was a bad burn, and I was in real fear that it might have an ill ending. He made light of it, however, and tried to keep up the child's spirits. I tried to help him, and she went to bed less unhappy than I expected. Macrae's strength and constitution stood to him, and, though the hand was badly scarred, he fully recovered its use.

'That night he was so feverish that I insisted on sitting up with him. I was able to give him some ease, and he was grateful for it. He talked with me more freely than he had ever done. He insisted on going several times to see how the child slept. He came back after one of these visits with his eyes wet, and as he lay down on his bed said softly:

'"Poor little mite! God forgive me if I was wrong; but I thought it best!" Then turning to me, he went on:

'"I suppose you thought me not merely brutal, but fiendish. But if you knew how deeply for her own future happiness I value truth, you would perhaps be tolerant with me. It was a lie that ruined her mother's life and my own; and I would guard her against such an evil. Her mother and I loved each other, and there seemed no flaw in our lives; but once when in danger of death as we were rushing through a seething flood, she confessed to me that the innocence which had charmed me at the first was but an acted lie; that she had loved another man before she had seen me, and had lived with him guiltily. But, there! that page of my life is closed for ever." He said no more, and, of course, I never referred to the subject again. It struck me afterwards as strange that two people whom I had met had each suffered from a similar cause - as I myself had suffered - but it never struck me to connect them.

'After that night we became better friends, for we seemed to understand each other. I grew to love the child almost as much as if she had been my own daughter. During all that time I worked hard, and had few distractions; but I promised myself a treat when I should go over to Warrow,[14] the nearest town beyond the Creek,

---

14 There appears to be no Warrow in Victoria (or New South Wales, for that matter). Most probably Stoker invented the name, though there is a Warragul, some fifty miles east of Melbourne beyond Berwick, a railway town on the route to Cape Howe. Judging from the detailed timetables in *Dracula*, Stoker was a railway buff, as he had to be in his

for I had heard from Nurse Dora that she had become matron of the hospital there. The time which I had promised myself for my holiday was at hand, when little Dora fell ill of a fever. The white woman who was with us got it at the same time, and Macrae and I had to do the nursing ourselves. The floods[15] were out, and the Creek was like a sea; the natives, seeing a fever in the house, ran away. It was a quick fever, though a low one, and in a few days the woman died. The child got worse and worse, and her moaning was pitiful to hear. The father used to sit hour after hour with his head in his hands and groan. One evening I heard him say that if we had a woman to nurse her she might be saved; and this gave me an idea. I said nothing except that I was going out for a bit, for my mind was made up that I would try to fetch my friend the matron. I took my mare, Wild Meg, and swam the flooded Creek; and early in the morning, riding for all I was worth, fetched up at Warrow.[16] I went to the hospital and asked for the matron. When she came my heart leaped, and something within me seemed to cry out. It was as though two ends of an electric current were come together. Little Dora's fever-wasted face, as I had seen it the night before on the pillow, was reproduced in the pale lineaments of her who stood before me. I understood it all now. The man with the story; the woman with the story; the child parted from the mother; the mother who lied! Heaven had sent at the moment me, who, coming across the world, held in his hand the two ends of this chain of destiny. I told her of the child who was ill, dying; she wept, but said her duty held her to her post. Then I described the child and the solitary man, and a quick light leaped to her eyes. Hope had dawned in that withered heart! She said not a word, but with a gesture to me to wait, disappeared behind the hospital. In a minute she reappeared, leading by the bridle a magnificent roan[17] horse.

'"Come!" she said, and sprang to the saddle.

---

capacity as business manager at the Lyceum. If Stoker did have a real place in mind, the 'creek' would be either La Trobe or Tanjil – they merge – small rivers that are crossed by the railway.

15 The rains are torrential at the end of summer in an area which turns dry creeks into angry waters.

16 This is a hard ride, assuming Macrae's homestead was in the location of Moe and Lake Victoria, close on forty miles away.

17 A dark-coloured horse with light spots or of mixed colour with a reddish tinge.

'We rode all day without a word. Late in the afternoon we struck the creek, just as a thunderstorm came on, which in a moment lashed the flood into a raging torrent. But nothing daunted her. She rode boldly into the water, I following, and together we battled the watery element. Through danger and toil we won the further shore, though our two gallant steeds fell dead within sight of the house.[18] We hurried in, she leading, I following. When she stood in the doorway Macrae rose to his feet with a wild cry:

'"Dora, Dora, my darling, come at last! Now the child must live!" Then he fell fainting on the floor.'

Mr Sparbrook paused and looked round. Some of the women-kind were wiping their eyes, and sniffed, their bosoms heaving. Some of the men said 'Hear! hear!' feebly. The only audible remark was the comment of the Wardrobe Mistress:

'Mr Bloze is a-goin' of it this evening. He'll be a-puttin' of it into a ply. Him in Australiar! W'y, I've known 'im since 'e was a nipper, which 'is mother 'ad a puddin' shop at Ipswich[19] close along of the theyatre, an' 'e never was hout of England in 'is life!'

'You're next on the list,' said the MC to the Second Heavies,[20] Mr Hemans, who was sipping his hot grog with a preternaturally solemn look and manner.

'I know it, alas! I pity you all; but duty must be done. I suppose it is not necessary that *I* wander into the fields of romance?' – this with a covert look at the last story-teller.

'You give us fact, old man!' said the MC. 'After the heroics, a little sordid realism won't come amiss. If you could manage to tell us something funny we should all be grateful.'

'Anything in the shape of a Dead Byby?' he asked, with his face for one instant illumined by a humorous twinkle in his eye.

---

18 This is not surprising, given the length of their journey at full gallop.

19 Ipswich, in east Suffolk, is about seventy miles north east of London. A pudding shop was where you could buy 'take-away' pies and meat puddings.

20 In this period many dramas came close to melodramatics. A company would therefore employ character actors with fullness of body to assist the vocal resonance required for the necessary histrionics. They were termed First or Second Heavies. Such performers today would be considered 'ham' actors.

'Lydies and gents, not forgettin' of you, Mr Benville Nonplusser, sir, whenever ye likes I'm ready to go on with the 'arrowin' tyle of the Dead Byby what I eluded to before if –' She was cut short by the Second Heavies, who had no intention of being 'queered'[21] at the start by this species of realism:

'No dead babies in mine, thank you; but I was going to tell you of a somewhat humorous episode of a live baby – I may say a very-much-alive baby.'

'Hear! hear!' 'Silence!' 'Hus-s-sh!'

'Next!' said the MC to the Second Heavies, who was ready to begin:

'Some of you may perhaps know that I was not always an actor! That I am not one even now,' he added quickly, seeing the Tragedian[22] take his pipe from his lips preparatory to making a caustic comment. 'Having had aspirations towards the stage, and in especial towards high tragedy, I naturally became a commercial traveller, for I thought that self-possession and sheer, unadulterated, unmitigated impudence were the qualities which I ought to cultivate most assiduously!'

'Look here,' said the Tragedian, half rising from his seat. Seeing, however, no sympathy in the faces of the Company, he sat down again and smoked hard. The Second Heavies went on:

'From that I graduated into the undertaking business, for I soon saw that lugubriousness was a still more important item of stock-in-trade if my ambition was ever to he materialised. It was strange, however, that in neither branch of tragic art did I succeed. The clients considered me as a "drummer"[23] too solemn, and suspected a levity of manner superimposed upon a lugubriety of appearance. I found the greater centres of civilisation slow to compete for my mature efforts. So, crossing the seas, I gradually drifted towards the Setting Sun, earning for a time a precarious livelihood by drumming in the neighbourhood of the Black Mountains a new "Curative Compound"[24] calculated to obviate equally the ravages of sunstroke or frost-bite.

---

21 'queered': having his story spoiled.

22 The leading character actor specialising in tragic roles.

23 Insincere, as with many commercial travellers concerned only with making a sale.

24 He maybe became one of the infamous 'medicine-men' of the Wild West.

9

Chin Music

'ONE night we were journeying in the west of the Rockies[1] over a road bed[2] which threatened to jerk out our teeth with every loosely-laid sleeper on the line.

'Travelling in that part of the world, certainly in the days I speak of, was pretty hard. The travellers were mostly men, all over-worked, all over-anxious, and intolerant of anything which hindered their work or interfered with the measure of their repose. In night journeys the berths in the sleeping cars were made up early, and as all the night trains were sleeping cars, the only thing to be done was to turn in at once and try and sleep away the time. As most of us were tired out with the day's work, the arrangement suited everybody.

'The weather was harsh; sneezing and coughing was the order of the day. This made the people in the sleeper, all men, irritable: all the more that as most of them were contributing to the general chorus of sounds coming muffled through quilts and curtains, it was impossible to single out any special offender for general execration. After a while, however, the change of posture from standing or sitting to lying down began to have some kind of soothing effect, and new sounds of occasional snoring began to vary the monotony of irritation. Presently the train stopped at a way station;[3] then ensued a prolonged spell of shunting backwards and forwards with the uncertainty of jerkiness which is so peculiarly disturbing to imperfect sleep; and then two newcomers entered the sleeper, a man and a baby. The baby was young, quite young enough to be defiantly ignorant and intolerant of all rules and regulations regarding the common good. It played for its own hand alone, and as it was extremely angry and gifted with exceptionally powerful lungs,

---

1 The Rocky Mountains in the west of the United States extend northwards into Canada.

2 A loosely made rail track that runs adjacent to the main highway.

3 A junction where carriages are rearranged, added to, or uncoupled.

the fact of its presence and its emotional condition, even though the latter afforded a mystery as to its cause, were immediately apparent. The snoring ceased, and its place was taken by muttered grunts and growls; the coughing seemed to increase with the renewed irritation, and everywhere was the rustling of ill-at-ease and impotent humanity. Curtains were pulled angrily aside, the rings shrieking viciously on the brass rods, and faces with bent brows and gleaming eyes and hardening mouths glared savagely at the intruder on our quiet, for so we now had tardily come to consider by comparison him and it. The newcomer did not seem to take the least notice of anything, but went on in a stolid way trying to quiet the child, shifting it from one arm to the other, dandling it up and down, and rocking it sideways.

'I took considerable amusement, myself, from the annoyance of my fellow-passengers. I had no cold myself, and so had been worried by their discomforting sounds; besides, I had come to the car from a dinner with clients, where the wine of the country had circulated with quite sufficient freedom. When a man has a large family – I regret to say that at that time my first wife was nursing her seventh – he acquires a certain indifference to infantile querulousness. As a matter of fact, he does not feel sympathy with the child at all, his pity being reserved for other people.

'All babies are malignant;[4] the natural wickedness of man, as elaborated at the primeval curse, seems to find an unadulterated effect in their expressions of feeling.

'I confess that the sight of a child crying, and especially crying angrily – unless, of course, it disturbs me in anything I may be doing – affords me a pleasure which is at once philosophical, humorous, contemplative, reminiscent and speculative.'

'Oh, Mr Hemans, how horrid you are to say such things!' said the Leading Lady. 'You know you don't think anything of the kind. There's no one who loves little children better than you do, or who is so considerate to them!' He made no reply, but only held up a hand in protest, smiling sweetly as he resumed:

---

4 An extraordinarily cynical vision of childhood but obviously intended here as attention-grabbing black humour.

'This baby was a peculiarly fine specimen of its class. It seemed to have no compunction whatever, no parental respect, no natural affection, no mitigation in the natural virulence of its rancour. It screamed, it roared, it squalled, it bellowed. The root ideas of profanity, of obscenity, of blasphemy were mingled in its tone. It beat with clenched fist its father's face, it clawed at his eyes with twitching fingers, it used its head as an engine with which to buffet him. It kicked, it struggled, it wriggled, it writhed, it twisted itself into serpentine convolutions, till every now and then, what with its vocal and muscular exertions, it threatened to get black in the face. All the time the stolid father simply tried to keep it quiet with eternal changes of posture and with whispered words, "There, now, pet!" "Hush! lie still, little one." "Rest, dear one, rest!" He was a big, lanky, patient-looking, angular man with great rough hands and enormous feet, which he shifted about as he spoke; so that man and child together seemed eternally restless.

'The thing appeared to have a sort of fascination for most of the men in the car. The curtains of a lot of berths were opened, and a lot of heads appeared, all scowling. I chuckled softly to myself, and tried to conceal my merriment, lest I should spoil the fun. No one said anything for a long time, till at last one wild-eyed, swarthy, long-bearded individual, who somehow looked like a Mormon Elder,[5] said:

'"Say, mister! What kind of howling-piece is it you have got there? Have none of you boys got a gun?"

'There came from the bunks a regular chorus of acquiescence: "The durned thing had ought to be killed!"

'"Beats prairie dogs in full moon!"

'"When I woke up with it howlin', thought I had got 'em again."

'"Never mind, boys, it may be a blessin' in disguise. Somethin' bad is comin' to us on this trip, an' arter this 'twill[6] be easy work to die!"

'The man spoke up:

'"I'm sorry, gentlemen, if she incommodes you!" The words were so manifestly inadequate that there was a roar of laughter which

---

5 Religious Father of the Latter-Day Saints of Utah.

6 'and after this it will'.

seemed to shake the car. West of the Mississippi things are, or at any rate they used to be, a bit rough, and ideas followed suit. Laughter, when it came, was rough and coarse, and on this occasion even the lanky man seemed to feel it. He only tried to hold the child closer to him, as if to shield it from the hail of ironical chaff which followed.

'"Incommode us! Oh, not at all. It's the most soothing concourse of sweet sounds I ever heard."

'"Bully for baby syrups!"

'"Pray, don't let us disturb the concert with our sleeping."

'"Jerk us out a little more chin-music!"[7]

'"There's no place like home with a baby in it."

'Just opposite where the man moved restlessly with the child was the bunk of a young giant whom I had noticed turning in earlier in the evening. He had not seemed to have noticed the disturbance, but now his curtains were thrust aside fiercely and he appeared, lifting himself on one elbow, and he asked in an angry tone:

'"Say you, where's its mother, anyhow?" The man replied in a low, weary tone, without looking round:

'"She's in the baggage-car, sir – in her coffin!"

'Well, you could have heard the silence that came over all the men. The baby's screaming and the rush, and roar, and rattle of the train seemed unnatural breakers of the profound stillness. In an instant the young man, clad only in his under-flannels,[8] was out on the floor and close to the man.

'"Say, stranger," he said, "if I'd knowed that, I'd a bit my tongue out afore I'd 'a spoke! An' now I look at you, my poor fellow, I see you're most wore out! Here, give me the child, and you turn into my bunk an' rest. No! you needn't be afeered"[9] – for he saw the father shrink away a little and hold the child closer. "I'm one of a big family, an' I've nursed the baby often. Give her over! I'll take care of her, an' I'll talk to the conductor, and we'll see that you're called when the time comes." He put out his great hands and lifted

---

7 Vocal sounds. Howling with the mouth open.

8 One-piece full-length red flannel underwear, worn from the beginning of winter until the spring, by which time it was pretty ripe.

9 A snippet of Shakespearean English ('afraid') that has not changed over the centuries in many parts of America.

the little one, the father resigning her to his care without a word. He held her in one arm whilst with the other he helped the newcomer into his empty berth.

'Strange to say, the child made no more struggle. It may have been that the young blood or the young flesh gave something of the warmth and softness of the mother's breast which it missed, or that the fresh, young nerves soothed where the worn nerves of the sorrowing man had only irritated; but, with a peaceful sigh, the little one leaned over, let its head fall on the young man's shoulder, and seemingly in an instant was fast asleep.

'And all night long, up and down, up and down, in his stockinged feet, softly marched the flannel-clad young giant, with the baby asleep on his breast, whilst in his bunk the tired, sorrow-stricken father slept – and forgot.'

There was a long pause, with here and there a sniffle, whilst down the faces of many the tears trickled. The first to speak was the Leading Lady. Her face was as a masque of tender feeling, and the yearning of her voice went straight to every heart:

'That mother's body may have been far distant from where her baby and her husband slept, but somehow I think that her soul was not very far away.'

Again there was a long pause, broken by the Low Comedian:

'So that's what you call a funny story! A pretty bally funny story it is, to make us feel like this. Look at me!' His eyes were all blurred with crying. The next remark was made by the Sewing-Woman, a question asked with much anxiety:

'Did the Byby die, sir?'

And then everyone else in the saloon burst into a roar of laughter; the pent-up feelings of all had found a vent. The Second Heavies looked around with a complacent smile on his solemn face as he remarked:

'If it wasn't funny, what in thunder are you all laughing at?'

'I think you are next, my dear,' said the MC to the Singing Chambermaid.

'Oh, I do wish someone would go on for me,'[10] she protested with a pretty embarrassment, or what was an excellent assumption of the same. 'I do feel so bashful!'

'That being a condition antecedent to soubrette[11] success!' interrupted the Tragedian. She smiled at him with a helpless little simper, and went on:

'Couldn't you give my understudy[12] a chance?'

'Not me!' answered the latter quickly, 'I don't mind winging a part[13] when there's an accident; but you had your part in good time, and now, if you're not letter-perfect, you must do your own fluffing!'[14]

'Quite right, too!' said the Prompter, who was not, as a rule, attached to understudies.[15] The Manager nodded approval, so the Singing Chambermaid, with an appealing look round the Company, went on:

---

10 'go on for me', as on a stage, and play my part.

11 In this context a maid-servant in a comedy.

12 In all companies all performers in a play are 'covered' by a lesser actor in case of illness or accident.

13 Performing the part half-learned.

14 'fluffing': failing through nerves or faulty memory to perform an exact rendition of the script. It is always noticed by fellow members of the cast and usually by the audience.

15 Because of their inexperience and subsequent nerves, understudies required even closer attention to the 'book' by the Prompter.

10

A Deputy Waiter

'WHEN I began my career, I was ambitious to shine upon the lyric stage – no, sir! not in Shaftesbury Avenue.'[1] The interpolation was in answer to the Tragedian's again removing his pipe from his lips, preparatory to some effort of biting sarcasm. I intended Grand Opera, the whole big thing. I didn't take much stock of Comedy in those days. Indeed, I thought Comedy was vulgar!' Here there was an approving grunt from the Tragedian. Without turning to him she went on:

'As vulgar as tragedy was ridiculous! You needn't laugh, boys and girls – that was when I was young – very young; I know better about both things now.

'Well, they said at the Conservatoire[2] in Paris that I might succeed if a something-or-other happened to my throat, and that in such case I would be a star, for my voice would be abnormally high. However, the something-or-other didn't come off, and I had to look for success in a different way. I didn't know at that time that I had latent those gifts of Comedy and humour which have since then lifted me to my present height in my career. This is all nothing, however; it is only to explain how I came to be an intimate friend of the great cantatrice,[3] Helda, who was a class-fellow of my own. She went up like a rocket, if you like; and the stick never fell till it fell into her grave! In all her success she never forgot me, and whenever she knew I was in the same town, or near it, she always had me to come and stay with her. It was sometimes a nice change for me, too, for things were up-and-down with me. She was a good creature, and was able to take, in a lordly sort of way, all the honours that were showered upon her. But they must have oppressed her now and again; for when I would come to her she would love to pretend that

---

1 Shaftesbury Avenue in the West End of London runs from Piccadilly to Cambridge Circus. Then, as now, it was considered the heart of theatreland.

2 First training ground for 'serious' singers in Paris.

3 Female solo singer in cantatas, choral works often on a secular theme.

I was the great star, and would make me sit opposite her at dinner, or at supper after the play, when we were alone, all hung over with the magnificent jewels that Kings and Queens had given her. I liked it all at first, but after a few years, when the hollowness of the world had been burned into me, I began to feel it in my inmost heart as a bitter sort of mockery. Of course, I wouldn't have let her know my feeling for the world, for it would have cut her to the quick; so there was never any change, and the old girlish game went on to the end.

'It was when I was with her in Chicago that I had an adventure of an odd kind. Some of you may have heard of it?'

She looked round interrogatively; the silence was broken by the voice of the Tragedian:

'They've forgotten it, my dear, those who haven't become doddery[4] since then!'

'Bones, when you counter, even a woman,[5] you shouldn't hit below the belt!' said one of the young men, who had been at Oxford. The Tragedian glared at him, the appalling impudence of the youngster, who looked angry, and seemed to mean what he said, being unprecedented. A Young Man to put a Tragedian to rights! Of all the –! He felt, however, that he was in the wrong, and remained silent, waiting. The Singing Chambermaid looked saucily round her; but there was a tremble in the curl of her lips, and a furtive dimness as of unshed tears in her eyes. The blow had told. She went on:

'It is long ago; there is no denying that! But it seems to me all as clear as if it were yesterday! There was I, all alone, in Helda's flat. It was in the Annexe,[6] where there are suites of rooms with an outer door on the corridor with a regular latch-key.[7] Helda was singing in

---

4 Shaking, perhaps senile. The Singing Chambermaid is of mature age.

5 'even a woman'. Stoker segregates the sexes again.

6 Presumably part of the Chicago Opera House complex which opened in 1865 with Bellini's *La Sonnamblea*. The theatre burnt down in 1871.

7 Communal front door outside the theatre proper not controlled by the Stage Door keeper.

Fidelio,[8] and her maids were with her. I had stayed at home, because I was "under the weather," to use an Americanism, and I wasn't in *The Fatal Legacy*, which our company was giving that night at McVicker's. I was lying back in a comfortable chair, half dozing, when I heard the door open with a latch-key. I didn't turn round, for there was a special waiter who attended each suite, and I thought he had come to ask if I wished for coffee, as he usually did about that time when we were at home. It seemed as if at the same time the housemaid had gone in to make up the bedrooms. He did not speak to me as usual, so I said sleepily:

'"Fritz." There was no answer.

'"I think, Fritz," I said, "I would like a cup of tea to-night, instead of coffee." He still said nothing, so I looked round, and saw that it was a strange waiter. "Oh," I said, "I thought it was Fritz. Where is he?" The man answered me with perfect politeness:

'"He has gone out, madam! This is his night off, but I am to take his place."

'"Then," I said, "will you kindly bring my tea as soon as you can. I have a headache, and it may do it good." I sank back in my chair again. I did not hear him go out, so I looked round and said: "Do pray make haste," for his waiting irritated me. He had not stirred, but stood there looking at me fixedly. I began to feel a bit frightened, for there was, I thought, a wild look in his eyes as of a man hunted or desperate. In Helda's room I heard the rustle of the chambermaids at their work. I rose quickly and went towards the door, intending to join them and then get somebody else sent up instead of the new waiter, who was, I had by this time settled in my mind, mad. Just, however, as my hand was on the door-knob, a voice behind me, thin and keen, said in a fierce whisper:

'"Stop!" I turned round and looked straight into the muzzle of a revolver pointed at my head. For an instant I was too paralysed to scream out, and then I felt that the only way to deal with a madman was to be calm and cool. Let me tell you, however, that being calm and cool under certain conditions is no easy task. I would just then have given my year's salary to have been able to have appeared hot and flustered. The voice came again:

---

[8] The opera by Beethoven.

'"Sit there! His hand pointed to the piano stool. I sat down. Again came the voice:

'"I know you; you are a Singing Chambermaid! Sing!"

'In the midst of all my trouble it was some comfort to find my professional abilities recognised, even by a lunatic.[9] When I looked at him to ask what I should sing, I saw his eyes roll horribly. I thought it better not to ask questions, so I started at once my great song, "George's Kiss is not like Daddy's," which I had rendered famous in the Farce-Comedy, *From the West.* At first he did not seem to like it. Some of you may have heard it – of course, in your extreme youth' – this with a reproachful look at the Tragedian. 'It begins wonderingly, and then works up and up with each verse. It is a song that has to be acted, and in those days I used to finish the refrain with a high note, a sort of suggestion of sudden surprise as one gives at an unexpected pinch. The "Inter-ocean"[10] called it "Miss Pescod's yelp." The boys in the gallery used to take it up, and the latter verses were always chorused by the audience.[11]

'My lunatic friend had evidently not heard the song, though I had been singing it three times a week in Chicago for a whole month, so I guessed that, as he knew me as an actress, he must have seen me in some other town. He entered into the spirit of the thing, however, and when he heard the end of the first verse his face relaxed, and he cried, "Hear! Hear!" Thenceforward he made me sing the refrain of every verse over several times, and joined in the chorus himself. He seemed to be satisfied with my complaisance, for though he held the revolver in his hand, he did not keep it pointed at me.

'In the middle of one of the verses the door from the bedroom opened very slightly and so softly that, had I not seen it, I should not have known; the maids were evidently listening. This was my

---

9 A true theatrical reaction. Never mind the dilemma, so long as my correct 'billing' is observed.

10 This is presumably Stoker's fictional Chicago newspaper.

11 This was the custom in Stoker's time, especially in 'front-cloth' solos. A front cloth is a 'drop-down' curtain with a full scene painted on it – a street, perhaps, or landscape. The artiste performed in front of it, in a small space before the footlights with no other props or furnishings, while the next scene was being prepared behind the cloth. This tradition continued into the 20th century in Music Halls, such as the Players Theatre, London.

chance; I called out imperatively and sharply:

'"Come in!"

'The door was instantly shut – so quickly that this time it sounded loudly; at the same instant the muzzle of the revolver rose and covered me.

'"Silence!" came the fierce whisper. "This treat is for me alone! It is death to someone if it be shared!" I tried to go on singing, but the sudden terror was too much for me. I put my hands to my forehead to steady myself. At that instant I heard the lintel of the outer door click; the maids had evidently gone.

'I looked up at the waiter. He was grinning with a savage delight; and as I was now quite powerless, I sank to the floor. He said, with his eyes rolling:

'"Mine alone! All for me now! All the entrancing delight of music from a Master voice! Then he pointed the revolver at me, saying:

'"Get up, Singing Chambermaid! Sing! Sing to me! Sing for your life!"

'It is astonishing what a restorative a revolver, properly used, can be. I don't know but that when I have a theatre of my own I won't present one to my Stage Manager. It would be a prompt and admirable help!'

'Hear! Hear!' said the Stage Manager enthusiastically. She resumed:

'Well, I got up quickly and went on with the song just where I had left off. It didn't do to have any fooling around under the circumstances. I sang for all I was worth, and the lunatic joined in the chorus with a gleeful zest which was bewildering. I would like to have scratched him!

'When he had encored the whole song twice, I began to get tired. It was no joke to me; and if it hadn't seemed really a matter of life and death, I couldn't have gone on. When I made a protest, he scowled at me, and his hand rose with the revolver. After a moment's thought he said:

'"You can have five minutes' rest from singing, but you must go on playing."

'I began to play. I thought some merry tune might soothe him, and I started into a Scotch reel.[12] The effect was so far good that he began to snap his fingers and to keep time with his feet. All the time my brain was working, and it flashed across me that if I could move him thus to my will with music, I might be able to devise some means to rid myself of him. There was so much of hope in the thought that it almost overcame me, and I began to laugh. The instant my hands stopped, his moved, and the revolver rose again.

'"Play up, or you're lost!" came the peremptory whisper.

'Nature is nature, and necessity is necessity, and I suppose that hysterics is the result of the struggle between them. Anyhow, I kept playing away at the reel, and all the time rolling on the piano stool with laughing. Presently I was recalled by a peremptory word:

'"Time!" I looked round; the revolver still covered me. He went on:

'"The five minutes is up! Singing Chambermaid, do your work! Follow your vocation! Exercise your calling! Practise your art! Sing!"

'"What shall I sing?" I asked in desperation. His face wore a sardonic smile as he replied:

'"Sing the same song again. You will have time to think of something else whilst you are singing it!"

'I began the song again. I used to think it very funny, and full of a sort of quaint plaintiveness, but now it seemed only a mass of distressing rubbish – false sentiment, indelicate, inane. From that hour I could never sing it without a nauseating sense of humiliation.'

'Hear! Hear!' said the Tragedian, but drew back under the fierce 'Hsh' of the Company. The Singing Chambermaid looked at him reproachfully, and went on:

'Presently my lunatic waiter drew close to me, and whispered:

'"Don't stop! If you pause a moment you are a dead woman. Here is Fritz; I hear his footsteps." He must have had wonderful ears, I thought; but that is the way of madness. "When he opens the

12 This should perhaps read 'Scottish' not 'Scotch', which is whisky. A 'reel' is a lively traditional dance performed throughout northern Europe.

door, tell him that you are practising some songs, and don't want to be disturbed. Remember, I am watching you! If you even falter, your life and his are forfeit! I am desperate! The music is mine alone, and alone I will have it!" He withdrew to the bedroom, leaving the door slightly open. He could not be seen from the outer door, but he could see me. And I could see him, with his revolver pointed at my head, and a set, vindictive, threatening scowl upon his evil face. I knew that he would kill me if I did not do as he wished, so when Fritz opened the door, I called to him as complacently as I could – there is some use in stage training:

'I am practising, Fritz, and do not wish to be disturbed. I shall want nothing till Madame comes in.'

'"Goot!" said the pleasant Fritz, and he at once withdrew.

'Then my mad friend came out from the room, and said, showing his teeth with a grim smile:

'"You showed your nerve and your wisdom, Singing Chambermaid; now sing!"

'Well, I sang, and sang, and sang all the songs I could think of, till I grew so weary that I could hardly sit erect; and my brain began to reel. The maniac then began to grow more desperate. As I grew fainter he levelled his pistol at me and forced me to go on from very fear of death. His face began to twitch, his eyes to roll horribly, and his mouth to work convulsively as he called, in a fierce whisper:

'"Go on. Sing! Sing! Faster! Faster! Faster!"

'He made me go faster and faster still, beating time with the revolver, till my breath began to go. I held on in mortal fear till even sheer terror could no longer uphold me. The last thing I saw as I fell senseless from the stool was his scowling face and the bobbing muzzle of the revolver as he called, "Faster! Faster!"

'The next thing I remember is hearing Helda's voice, seemingly coming from a great distance. I recognised the tone before I heard the words, but things grew clearer and clearer, and at last I knew that it was her hands which held my head up. Then I heard distinctly the words she said:

'"Oh, don't bother! What does it matter? I would rather see her her dear self than all the jewels in Christendom!" Then came a gruff, strong voice:

'"But, look here, ma'am. Time is everything now! We can't begin till we get some kind of clue. Do you just tell us what you know; we'll do the rest.' She answered impatiently:

'"I really know nothing, except what I've told you already. I came in after the Opera, and found her here in a dead faint. Perhaps, when she regains her consciousness, she will be able to tell us something." Then came the strong voice again:

'"And you, Fritz Darmstetter, have you no more to say than this: 'I came several times during the evening, and heard her singing, generally the same song over and over again. Something about George and Daddy. When, at last, I opened the door, she told me to go away, as she was practising, and did not want to be disturbed. She would not want anything till Madame came"?'

'"Dat is so!" Here I seemed to become awake. I opened my eyes, and when I saw my dear Helda close to me, I clung to her and implored her to protect me. She promised me that she would. Then, somewhat reassured, I looked round and saw myself surrounded with a crowd. At one side was a row of gigantic policemen, with a still more gigantic inspector standing in front of them; on the other side were a lot of the hotel[13] servants, male and female, and Helda's maids, who were wringing their hands. One of the policemen carried Helda's Russia-leather jewel-case with the lid wrenched off. When the Inspector saw my eyes open he stooped and, with a sweep of his arm, lifted me to my feet.

'"Now," he said in a commanding voice, "now, young lady, tell me what you know!"

'I suppose we women know a man's voice when we hear it, and we, or our mothers before us, have learned to obey, so I spoke out instinctively:

'"The lunatic came in and pointed a revolver at me, and made me sing all the evening till I fell down with fatigue!"

'"What was he like, miss?" asked the giant Inspector in an imperative voice.

'"He was thin," I answered. "He had dark whiskers and a shaven upper lip, and his eyes rolled!" Then I proceeded to tell him all I knew of the lunatic's strange proceedings.

---

13 The 'Annexe' is now described as an 'hotel'.

'As I spoke, there came a queer sort of grin on the faces of the policemen; the Inspector seemed to voice their sentiments as he said:

'"Well, ma'am, this case is pretty clever. Guess its Dimeshow[14] Pete this time. The old man has fooled us all. He seems to have been tarnation[15] clever over it! That was a cute scheme of his to make the young woman sing over and over again the same song with the high note, like as she was practising, whilst his confederates got off with the swag. Guess they're off on the Lake Shore[16] special hours ago, and he's gone on the *Flyer*, and has jumped at Lake. Pete's a peach! He's been too many for us this time, but I reckon we'll chalk it up to him agin the time comes!"'[17]

For some little time the eyes of the Company had been gradually focussing the Tragedian, who was next in order. He had himself shown to experienced eyes a certain uneasiness, though he tried with all the wile of his craft to disguise it in a mantle of *dégagé*[18] self-possession.

When the last speaker had completely finished – this, his auditory being actors, being when the applause had entirely ceased and the opportunity for encore or recall had come and gone – the MC spoke:

'Now, Mr Dovercourt, we hope for the honour of hearing from you!' There was an immediate chorus from all the Company, the Manager being bland – not exactly patronising, but striking an exact mean between condescension and respect – whilst the rest all down the line with an ever-growing serious attention which began with the Low Comedian's companionable deference and ended with the Sewing Woman's self-abasement.

The latter, who through effluxion of time which had put her own literary effort in historical perspective, and influxion of the cup that cheers,[19] felt herself in a halo of imaginative glory, added her tearful request:

---

14 A dime is a tenth of a dollar, and refers to the cheapest theatrical show.

15 'tarnation': damnation. Here, damnably clever.

16 The Lake Michigan ferry.

17 'When his time comes.'

18 Unconstrained.

19 The lady was 'in her cups'. The whisky punch had inebriated her.

'And if I might make so hold, Mr Wragge, seein' as 'ow I may now claim to be myself a sister hartis,[20] though in a numble wy,[21] I would wenture to arsk if you could tell us out of tragic lore some instance of anythink which isn't about a dead byby, which the same belongs to my spear, an'' – this said with an air of vicious determination – 'I means to 'old to my rights, though I be a numble woman what knows her plyce for all the –'

Her eloquence was cut short by the MC, who said, with a stern determination which reached her intelligence through her somewhat clouded faculties:

'That will do, Mrs Wrigglesworth! When your turn comes again we'll call on you, never fear. In the meantime, you must not interrupt anyone else; more especially one whom we all respect and admire so much as we do our Tragedian, the glory of our Company, the pride of our calling, the perfected excellence of our Art. Mr Dovercourt, here is your very good health! Ladies and gentlemen all! in the good old fashion: Hip, Hip, Hurrah!'

The toast was drunk standing, and with a manifest respect on the part of all, which was a really effective tribute to his branch of his Art. Growl as they may, the companions of the Tragedian have always a secret respect, if not for the Man, at least for the Artist.

The Tragedian began:

---

20 Stoker anticipates Shaw's Professor Higgins, who is fascinated by the sounds of Eliza, and Dustman Dolittle's, 'murdering' of correct English.

21 'numble wy': humble way.

11
Work'us

'As my friend Parmentire said earlier in this symposium, the humour is not always to its – ah! professional exponent, the Comedian. It may somewhat mitigate the gloom in which the enactment of my special *rôles* in the greater passions for which opportunity has been given to me – and others – yes, to others – by the Master, Shakespeare, and the galaxy of dramatic, poetic talent which has carried down to our day the torch of tragic thought, if I, in this hour of social communion when, if I may be allowed the expression, the buskin is unlaced[1] and the sock is – ah! somewhat eased, relate to you a somewhat humorous episode of my "hot youth," when, like our dear Prince Hal,[2] I occasionally made the welkin[3] ring in its darker hours before the dawn.

'Looking back over the vista of time, those hours of revelry seem to have left a less effaceable mark on memory than does the whirlwind of jealous passion, or even the soft dalliance of the hours of love.'

'Oh, Mr Dovercourt!' said the Second Lady, putting up her fingers to screen a modest blush. The Tragedian, pleased, went on:

'It is, perhaps, the contrast between my hours within what I may call my art-workshop and those without its pale – what a great writer has called the "irony of things" – which makes my memory cling to little trivial absurdities of days long gone; whilst the same memory has lost sight of many an hour of paramount triumph, snatched from eager humanity even before the very thrones of the Kings of the Earth. Ah, me! those halcyon days[4] which are gone for

---

1 The ancient Tragedian's high, lace-up boot.

2 From Shakespeare's *Henry IV*, Parts One and Two. Prince Hal is Henry's son, to be glorified by Shakespeare in *Henry V*.

3 'welkin' is old English for 'sky'. This line therefore is interpreted as: 'make the sky ring with the sound of his voice.'

4 'halcyon days': calm times. From a fabled bird said to have power to calm the seas at the winter solstice in order to nest upon the waters.

aye![5] But "sit still my soul" and "break my heart, for I must hold my tongue."[6] Well, it was when I was in the stock at Wigan,[7] when Hulliford Greenlow controlled the theatrical destinies of that home of the black diamond.[8] A few of us choice spirits were used as a habit to assemble nightly when our work at the theatre was over. Our rendezvous was at the hotel, or rather I should say the public-house, known as "The Merry Maiden." It was in reality but a drinking house; but there were a few bedrooms which were now and again occupied by some overcome reveller. The place, however, had so bad a reputation in the eyes of the police that no one would willingly remain in it after the withdrawal of the extraneous company, unless quite overcome by his libations to Bacchus.[9] Naturally our conversation, if at times pronounced, was bright; and naturally, too, there were at times jokes, both practical and - and - ah - verbal, consonant with the various dispositions of the nightly frequenters of the house. There were a few choice spirits who were outsiders to our habitual galaxy, and efforts were often made by others to penetrate our charmed circle. We were, however, conservative in our tendencies. We cared for none of the guests who were not good company; and the landlord, a genial soul but thoroughly equipped with business instincts, did not care for any company which was devoid of surplus cash. Naturally the more choice spirits amongst us had at times periods of - ah - petrifaction, when, in fact, the ghost had not walked;[10] and at such times we were wont to reap in a practical shape the harvest of which the seed-time had been a certain toleration extended to repetition on the part of some of our eclectic community, and the exercise of some of our histrionic talents in enacting the part of listeners.[11]

---

5 'gone for ever'.

6 From the first soliloquy of *Hamlet* lamenting on his dead father.

7 'in a repertory company in Wigan, Lancashire'.

8 'black diamond': coal.

9 This is unlikely to be a tribute to the libations of Bacchus, the young Greek God of wine. Then and now the 'public house' wine would be cheap and probably undrinkable. Stoker is more likely to be referring to gin, or beer - perhaps 'Porter', a dark sweet ale brewed from black malt.

10 The 'ghost' usually walked on Fridays. This is a theatre expression meaning the management had paid the salaries. Or, in this case, had not.

11 When you listen you are someone else's guest. So he pays the bill.

'One night we had a strange experience in the shape of a fresh guest. He was a very young man, a weakling and somewhat deformed. In fact, our genial host called our attention at first to his - ah - eccentricity by the humorous way in which he addressed him as "my lord,"[12] it being our custom in those days to designate as a nobleman anyone whom Dame Nature had in a malevolent moment inflicted with a curvature of the spine.[13] The youth was ill at ease, but he was so manifestly ambitious to share our revelry, and he was so eager in his appreciation of our merry quips and cranks - the flashing by-play of our intellectual swords - that we decided tacitly to allow him to remain amongst us. Our humorous but business-like host took care that the new-comer's expenditure on the goods of his trade was commensurate with his enjoyment. On further visits of this young nobleman he so harassed him into needless expenditure - an expenditure manifestly ill according to his means, for his garments were poor and worn - that one or two of our duller spirits interfered, and chid[14] our host into a more decorous observance of the economic proprieties. The youth would join us at irregular periods, but seldom a week passed that he did not make his appearance. After a little his shyness wore away, and now and again he ventured to make a remark, generally of an abstruse kind and necessitating for its full understanding an intimate acquaintance with the classics.[15] By this time, too, we had come to know something of the youth's personal surroundings. He was the son of a man who had been a teacher in a school, but who had been killed at a fire whilst he was helping at a rescue. His widow, being penniless, had, of course, to go to the Union,[16] where the boy was brought up. Being a cripple and unable to play or work with other boys, he had been allowed to take advantage of the

---

[12] This is an extraordinary confession by Mr Dovercourt. He may well be a talented performer, but offstage he is a vicious little man and here like attracts like.

[13] Less politely, the boy was a hunchback.

[14] 'chid': chide. Rebuked.

[15] By 'classics', Dovercourt implies Shakespeare and the Elizabethans, a common error among the 'Actor-Laddie' school of performer. Though the boy may have studied the 'Dead' languages, the Tragedian most likely knew his Greeks and Romans through the verse-dramas of contemporary poet-dramatists, unless taught by his teacher father.

[16] Parishes administering the poor-laws, and workhouses erected by such. Another common expression was 'on the Parish'.

school, and had read all the books he could get and had taught himself some of the dead languages. When these facts had come to our knowledge, some of our community were not well pleased that he should have come amongst us. There is, Ladies and Gentlemen, a very natural prejudice against the workhouse taint,[17] and some of the high-spirited members of our little coterie resented it. Our genial host was one of the most indignant. He was, though himself a man of humble origin, one of very fine feelings, and he said it hurt him, and it hurt his house, to be tainted with any workhouse scum – such was the humorous way in which he expressed himself.[18] "To think," said he, "of his damned impudence, comin' 'ere to my 'ouse – my 'otel – a-spendin' of money while 'is hold mother is a-livin' in the workus, kep' by rates paid by you an' me. I'll let 'im know what I thinks before I've done with 'im." The man who had told us the story set the landlord right upon one point; the old lady was not living in the Union, nor had been for some time. So soon as her son had begun to earn money, which he did, it was said, by writing for papers and magazines, he had taken her out, and they lived together in a tiny house some distance outside the town, where rent was cheap.

'Well, we were discussing the affair, when "lo! and behold you" –'

'My hown words! 'E's a-stealin' of 'em from me!' came from the Sewing Woman, with a snort. 'H-ss-sh!' went round the company. The Tragedian glared, and went on:

'When lo! and behold you, who should come in but the very hunchback himself in a new suit of clothes. We all tried to look as if there was nothing strange; but do what we would, the conversation from that moment on kept about nothing else than the workhouse. Our genial host did not say a word, from which I gathered that he had some deep design. At first the young man coloured up and

---

17 This 'taint' would be marked among snobs like Dovercourt. Actors are not necessarily well educated. If they have a collective fault it is that they are blinkered by the topic of theatre. And themselves first in relation to it.

18 Humorous! This is the very essence of inverted snobbery. His 'morality' does not stop him fleecing the young man at every opportunity.

flushed something painful to see; but presently he went over to the bar and gave an order *sotto voce*. Then he came back amongst us, and, standing up, said something like this:

'"Gentlemen, I want you all to drink a bowl of punch[19] with me. To-night is a red-letter night[20] with me, and I want you all, good fellows that you are, to let me speak my gratitude to you. For you have done for me more than you perhaps know. You let me come amongst you and share all your fun, and get inspiration from your brilliancy. I feel most keenly all you have just been saying about the workhouse. No one knows better than I know how true it all is. But I owe it something; I owe it much. It sheltered my mother in her trouble, and it sheltered me in my youth. It gave me education, and made thus for me possibilities which I might not otherwise have had. And, indeed, I am grateful to it. But the life there is a barren one at best, and there is little light through its dull, sad shade. I wanted a contrast to this shade of my youth, and I heard someone speak of you fellows and your brighter evenings here. I was earning but little money, but the schooling which my mother and I had gone through made our wants but few, and I was able to save each week the necessary sum to pay my footing here. My dear mother wished it. She used to sit up for me till I returned whenever I came here; and before we went to bed I told her of you all and most of the clever things I had heard. Then out of all your brightness, and with the contrast to what I knew already, I found I could begin the play I had longed to write. You gave me material! You gave me inspiration! You gave me hope! And I wish you could know the depth of gratitude in my heart. My play is to be rehearsed to-morrow at the Crown Theatre[21] in London, and I am to be there to help. I got some little money only yesterday for a story, and you see me in the first good suit of clothes I ever had. I tell you all these things because you have been so good to me that I want you to feel, one and all, how much I owe you. This shirt I wear, my mother made herself and washed and ironed for me; and it touched me

---

19 The Dickensian drink of spirits or wine with lemon and spices usually drunk hot.

20 In almanacs and ecclesiastical calendars important dates were printed in red. Hence they became known generally as special days.

21 There was a Crown Theatre in Peckham, south-east London, later known as the Peckham Hippodrome. It was demolished in the 1930s and replaced by a cinema.

when I was coming out to-night when she brought it to me and said: 'My boy, I can't be with you, but I want you to feel that I am near you. Every stitch in this is put in with love and hope, and you must feel it, whether you think of it or not.' It was she who counselled me to come here to-night to thank you all, my good friends; to close worthily the door on the old life, and bring, if I may, into the new life some of the good feeling that you have so freely given me in the old." He appeared moved, and the tears were in his eyes. We all drank his punch, of course; and as it was his punch we had, of course, to drink his health. Then, if you please, our genial host got up and said that he was going to stand a bowl of punch too, so that we might bid our young friend adieu. So we drank his punch also. Then he came and whispered to me to order another bowl of punch. "I'll pay for it. See that his Lordship drinks plenty; I mean to be even with Work'us!"[22] So the whisper went round the jovial spirits that our young friend was to have a skinful. And he had. He was not accustomed to such freedom of liquor, and after the first few glasses it wasn't hard to persuade him to drink more. He was always reminding us that he had to catch the train for London at 8.15, and he kept showing us his ticket.

'Then we put him to bed in a room of "The Merry Maiden." We all helped. But before we went away we took the gloss off that new suit of clothes. I daresay we were a bit rougher than was necessary; but it was so excruciatingly funny to think of when he would wake with a headache and find his new clothes torn and burned in holes, and stabbed with a penknife, and blotched with ink and candle-grease. Finally we put the shirt up the chimney and dragged it about the floor a bit till it was a real picture.[23] As we came away our genial host observed with a laugh: "'Lord Work'us' will find it like old times when he sees his clothes."

'Well, our little joke wasn't quite complete after all. We had, of course, intended that he should miss his train; but it seems that early in the morning his mother came looking for him, and learned from a servant that he was there. Our genial host was still asleep, so

---

[22] Workhouse.

[23] Strange to say, the Tragedian thinks this disgusting behaviour is funny, though many distinguished performers are notorious practical jokers.

there was no one to prevent her entering. I believe she just got him to the train in time. He hadn't a coin about him after he had paid for his bowl of punch.

'I heard from one of the Company at the Crown that he arrived in a terrible state. He was well plucked enough,[24] I will say that for him; and he would have gone on with his work looking like a scarecrow, only that by some evil chance Grandison, the Manager, saw him in time and took him away to his own room and let him wash and rigged him up.

'Anyhow, he never came back to Wigan. And now look at the justice of things! Here's this workhouse upstart with a fortune. They say he has over a hundred thousand pounds, his wife and his mother drive about in carriages; whilst men of genius like myself have to pig it in hovels with the riffraff of the stage. Pah!'[25]

He drowned the depth of his indignant emotion in his drink.

For a time no one spoke; the men smoked, the women looked down at nothing on their laps. The first sound heard was from the Engine-Driver:

'That's a funny story – a really funny story! I won't say what I think, because this is Christmas-time, and the gent who told it is an old one with one foot in the grave. I'm from Wigan, I am. So you can fancy how nice it is for me to hear a story like that. I know where "The Merry Maiden" is, and I know, too, the sort of reputation that the "genial host" bears. Bless him![26] I'll look in there when I'm next at home, and see if we can't fix up another joke of some kind!'

Later on he was heard to say in private conversation with the MC:

'Look here, mister, you're a man of the world. Tell me, how do the beaks[27] look nowadays on scrappin' in the Midlands? What do they consider a fair fine where there has been a holy shindy[28] and some hound has been wiped the floor with?'

---

24 Plucky. Brave enough.

25 It seems there is no limit to this ghastly man's ego.

26 Of course, this is irony. 'Bless' is not the word in the Engineer's thoughts.

27 'beaks': magistrates.

28 'shindy': fight. Someone gets a good hiding.

'You are next, Murphy,' said the MC, looking at the Super-Master,[29] and at the same time handing a glass of steaming whisky punch. 'Don't be afraid of this. 'Tis John Jamieson.'[30]

'I'm a timarious man be nature,' he answered as he began to sip the punch as a preliminary, 'but whin I'm dhragged into publicity like this I'm tuk be the short hairs,[31] so ye'll pardon me, I thrust, Ladies and Gents all, av I thransgress in me shortcomin's.' Being an Irishman, he was regarded by the Company as a humorist, and felt that he had to keep up that perilous reputation – just as he had to strain himself now and again to achieve a sufficient brogue.

'I suppose 't would be betther for me to shtay on dhry land an' to give an expayrence iv me own, rather than to be afther gettin' into difficulties be puttin' out to say what I don't know in the way of shtories an' consates.[32] *Illi robur et aes triplex circa pectus erat.*[33] Yous'll remimber!' He had been brought up at a hedge school,[34] and always advanced the preposterous statement that he had been 'at College.'

'All right, Murphy. What you will, but hurry up! This isn't Monday trunks, but Sunday hand-bags!'[35] The professional simile was received with laughter and applause by the actors; but Murphy, who was a shrewd fellow, knew too much to waste his opportunity on quips and cranks, so went on at once.

---

29 Stage management. In charge of the 'Supers', in other words non-speaking parts.

30 Stoker reverses the order of things. 'John Jamieson' is an Irish Single Malt whiskey but here 'whisky' is spelt as Scotch.

31 Usually the 'short and curlies'.

32 'shtories an' consates': stories and concerts.

33 'Oak and triple bronze must have girt the breast of that one'. From the *Odes of Horace*, Book 1, No 30, lines 9-10 (Loew's translation).

34 The hedge schools of Ireland have a fascinating history, being run 'illegally' by priest-tutors honing on Classical subjects and languages, against the wishes of their English educational masters. As Latin was part of the curriculum, the quote is in order. The schools came to an end with Daniel O'Connell's insistence that all Irish speakers learn English so they might become 'international'.

35 This is a theatrical joke, a play on words. Instead of the first costume to be worn, taken out of the trunk on Monday night, the line refers to Sunday-travel hand-luggage, light and easily sorted.

12

A Corner in Dwarfs

'I WAS Super-Master at the Lane Theatre[1] when the "Stage Children's Act"[2] was passed. I had to make it up a bit, for it was part iv me wurrk t' engage the kids as well as the exthras, an' it was a rare job that year, I can tell ye. Ould Gustavus[3] had quarrelled the year before with Madam Laffan, the dancin' misthress, iv Old Street, who used to take all the East-end childher,[4] an' Mrs Purefoy had made her fortune and retired, so there was no one west with a stock of trained kids. The Act, you remimber, was pushed through be the faddists, an' became law before anyone could wink. Then the throuble began. The parents what usually kem beggin' an' prayin' to have their kids took on began to trate[5] even me haughty, an' t' ask for conthracts. They wanted double an' tribble pay. They thought they had a right to sell their childher's services, and that the new law couldn't touch them. So ould Gustavus held off in turn, when, lo and behold! you –'

'He's stealin' my words too!' murmured the Sewing Woman under her breath. She didn't dare to speak out loud for fear of offending him. Murphy was a kindly creature, and often showed her small kindnesses.

'– the beaks[6] shut down on the whole thing, and wouldn't allow any childher at all to be engaged. We was all at our wits' end thin. We had for Pantomime[7] that Christmas *Cinderella*. It was to be all

---

1 The 'Theatre Royal, Drury Lane', actually fronts off Catherine Street. A series of famous theatres has existed on this site since 1662.

2 An Act of Parliament, restricting working hours, improving child conditions and requiring time set aside for education by chaperone-tutors.

3 In the 1880s and 90s the Theatre Royal was managed by Sir Augustus Harris, 'Ould Gustavus', who was known in the profession as 'Augustus Druriolanus'.

4 'childher': children.

5 'trate': treat.

6 'beaks': thieves' jargon for magistrates in the civil courts in the UK.

7 The Christmas Pantomime was the big attraction at Drury Lane.

done be childher, an' the scenery an' props an' costumes was all made. As time wint on I began to get anxious. Childher want a lot of tachin' an' dhrillin',[8] and av ye have to take 'em in the raw 'tis no light job. There ginerally is a lot of such about, and in usual circumstances – unless you have lift it too late – there does be plinty of the wans that have been on before, and have only to be freshened up and taught the business iv the new play. Av coorse, every thayatre has its own lists of thim what comes to be re-engaged – I think it only just to say that I'm not the only first-class Super-Master in the business! So by-an'-by, whin the Governor asked me how many kids I had engaged, I had to say to him:

'"Sorra a wan![9] Don't you remimber ye towld me not to engage a bally one – an' bally ind to me!"[10] Ould Gustavus was a man what niver got angry or swore or stamped about like some; but he had the nasty tongue on him that was a dale sight worse. So, sez he:

'"Oh, indade! Then, Mr Murphy, let me point out this to ye. If I've no supers an' no extras an' no childher, I don't seem to know that I have any use for a Super-Master – you undhershtand?"

'"I do!" sez I, an' wint out fit to hould. Whin I was shmokin' outside the stage-door,[11] the call-boy kem yellin' out:

'"Ye're wanted be the Guvernor, Murphy, at wanst."[12]

'Whin I kem in he says to me quite gintly – so gintly that I began to suspect he was up to some devilment:

'"Be the way, Murphy, in makin' any engagements, I want ye to put in yer own name as employer. It may be a good thing, ye know, for ye personally, an' 'twill make no differ to me."

'While he was shpakin'[13] I seen at a glance what he was up to – I think that quick. "Oh-ho!" sez I to meself, "that's the game, is it? 'Tis to be me what employs them! An' thin, whin the polis does be comin' along undher the new Act, 'tis the employer that has to be run in! ..."

---

8 'tachin' an' dhrillin'': teaching and drilling. This is still hard work for the producer, here the 'Super-Master'.

9 'Sorra a wan': not a one.

10 'bally ind to me': the blessed end to me.

11 Smoking was strictly forbidden inside the stage areas as a fire hazard.

12 Wanted by the boss at once.

13 'shpakin'': speaking.

'"May I have some forrms, surr?" I sez.

'"Certainly – as many as ye like. Take this ordher to Miles's an' get them to print ye a set." While he was shpakin', he tore out a forrm from th' ordher book, and handed it to me wid a conthract forrm which he had althered. "Tell them to print it like that – I have althered the name."

'"Thin, surr," I sez, "'tis me as employs them. I suppose I can do what I like in that way?"

'"Certainly, certainly," he sez. "You have a free hand in the matter. I shall make a contract with you when I want them."

'"An' their pay, sir?" I sez.

'"Oh, that is all right. You don't have to pay thim till work begins, ye know."

'"That's thrue!" sez I, an' wid that I wint out.

'I got me forrms from the printer next day – hundhreds, thousands iv them – an' set to worrk. I had a game av me own on, an' I tuk not a sowl[14] in me confidence. I knew 'twas no use gettin' childher at all, for whin the time'd come, the magisthrates wouldn't let thim wurrk at all, at all. So I luk'd round an' picked out all the small young weemen I could find that was nice an' shlim.

'My! but wasn't there a lot iv them. I had no idea that London was so full iv shlim young undher-sized weemen. I suppose I used to like big girrls best, and plazed me eye whin[15] I selected them. But there was I now engagin' the shmall wans be the score, be the hundhred, an' just whisperin' a word to aich iv thim to hould their tongues about their engagement, lest others'd crowd in an' kape thim out.[16]

'Thin I laid out some iv me own savin's in fares to all the big cities where they had pantomimes, an' I chose in the same way hundhreds iv shlim, short girls ivrywhere.

'Thin, whin I got back to London, I engaged, in Gustavus's name this time, a lot of kids for Misther Gustavus – rale childher this time. I had had a "*force majeure*" clause put in the conthract forrm in ordher to purtect him.

---

14 'sowl': soul.

15 'plazed me eye whin': pleased my eye when.

16 'kape thim out': keep them out.

'Ould Gustavus made his conthract wid me, agreein' to pay me for aich iv the childher[17] a shillin' a week more than usual. That was more than what I had agreed with their parents for; so in case there was no objections wid the polis they'd be betther off than usual. So that was all right.

'We began rehearsin' all right. An' wint on at it for two weeks: whin lo an' behold ye –'

'My words again!' murmured the aggrieved Sewing Woman.

'– down came the polis with a summons for ould Gustavus for contravenin' the Act be usin' on the stage the labour iv childher undher sixteen. He wint off to Bow Street[18] quite cocky, takin' me with him. For defince he said, in the first place, he wasn't employin' labour at all, for his theatre wasn't even open. An' in the second he wasn't the employer at all. It was me. But the magistrate shut him up short. He said he'd have him know that that was a quibble, as it was within his knowledge that I was in his employment on his staff, and that as I was his agent the legal maxim *facit per alium facit per se*[19] came in.

'"He's not me agent!" he says out loud. "An' look here, Murphy, I discharge ye on the shpot!"

'"That's enough," sez the magistrate. "Your dischargin' the man is a proof that he was yer agent up to that moment. Now the way you shtand is this. As this man Murphy was your agent, the childher were engaged be you; an' if y' allow them to appear in public you will go to prison. I accept the statement that they've not as yet been employed, as I understand that rehearsal is rather an unpaid preparation for employment than employment itself. I shall therefore discharge you to-day – or rather I shall postpone the hearing till afther Christmas. And, by the way, since you discharged this man summarily, you are, I take it, liable for a week's wages. You had betther pay him at once if you are wise! If not, an action will lie against you, and the proof will come from the Coort!"

---

[17] 'Each of the children.'

[18] The most famous London police station and magistrates court, directly opposite the Royal Opera House. The police station is now closed.

[19] In short, the employer is responsible for his staff.

'When we were in the street he sez to me:

'"Well?"

'"It looks like the end, surr, though it's only the beginnin'."

'"Of course, Murphy, I'll keep you on," he sez.

'"Thank ye, surr," sez I, "but I'm makin' other arrangements."

'"How do ye mane?" sez he.

'"I mane this, surr," sez I, "that ye've planted me for yer own purposes, an' now I intind that what grows out iv me plantin' is me own."

'"I don't undhershtand," sez he, "yit!"

'"Ye will by an' by," sez I. "Look here, Misther Gustavus, for yer own nefayrious[20] purposes ye tould me t' engage a lot iv childher for the pantomime, an' ye tould me t' ingage them in me own name. That was so that whin the polis'd come at ye ye might say, as ye done just now to the beak, that it wasn't you at all, but me. Now it was ayther you or me what engaged them be conthract. If 'twas you ye had to shtand the racket,[21] or would have done if the sayson[22] had begun – which it hadn't; an' ye'd have th' advantage, too. But ye said it wasn't you whin ye thought the polis had got ye, an' ye wanted to have me run in for it. So that's off. But if 'twas me what engaged thim, thin 'tis me what'll git the benefit. See? Moreover, ye discharrged me in the Coort, an' the beak himself said ye'd have to pay me me salary for a week. So now I'm free av ye, wid the kay iv the shtreet in me hand.[23] But I've got the conthracts what I've made wid a lot iv people in all kinds iv places. These are me own prawperty, an' I'm goin' to use thim in me own way. The only conthracts what is made in your name is wid the childher for yer own pantomime, an' thim ye has to shtand be. I might have tould his worship that they wor *your* conthracts, but I thought as ye swore at the beginnin' that they worn't I'd hould them over in case ye should git obstreperous later on.

'"So now ye're in the soup. Ye won't be let play the childher what ye engaged. An' I can tell ye now that ye won't be allowed any childhers at all, at all. But I've got meself in me own employment a

20 'nefayrious': nefarious, wicked.

21 'shtand the racket': face the consequences.

22 'if the sayson': if the season.

23 'Free of you with the key of the street in my hand.'

number iv likely young weemen iv shmall patthem what'll be able to play in shpite iv all the polis in the counthry. So av ye're wishful to git what ye want, Misther Gustavus, it's me that ye'll have t'apply to. I hould the whole shtock.[24] There is no use yer kickin'. I can prove me *bona fides* all along the line. 'Tis you what'll figure out as the bloated capitalist what deceived the poor honest workin' man – that's me – what thrusted him. What made nefayrious conthracts wid poor innocent childhers what'll have a hungry Christmas. An' what perjured hisself in a courthouse, which can be proved be the beak hisself an' some iv yer conthracts ye made wid the childher. Not be me, av coorse, for didn't ye swear that I was not in yer sarvice. But anyhow ye have got a *force majeure* clause in. That'll not look well, will it? As if 'twas I what put it in, whin I haven't the same clause even for me own purtection in me own conthracts."

'"So, Misther Gustavus, ye'd betther be quick in engagin' some iv me throup iv dancers.[25] I'll only charge double for sich iv thim what is took from me by me first pathron."

'Well, th' ould man was in a clift shtick, an' knew it. So he made me come back wid him to his office, an' then an' there made an iron-clad conthract wid me for the sarvices iv more'n a hundhred iv me dwarfs. "Mind ye," I had said to him, "ye can have as many as iver ye want at the price av ye take tham at wanst.[26] But if ye lave it over to take more later in case ye find ye've not enough, ye'll have to come in line wid the rest av the managers. No man can come in on the ground floor a second time!"

'It all kem off well. As soon as the rehearsals began the polis woke up an' got shpry[27] all over the counthry. The managers was all run in. Like ould Gustavus they couldn't be punished bekase they hadn't done nothin' wrong, as yet. But they tuk fright, as was intended, an' gave undhertakins not to employ any childher at all while th' Act run. An' so they all had to come, in the long run, to me what had cornered all the dwarfs. Mind ye, I was careful not to use that word, for if they'd any iv them heard it, they'd have riz up an' flew away like a flock iv pigeons does, all about nothin'.

---

24 'Hold the whole stock,' (of bona fides, guarantees.)

25 'Troupe of dancers.'

26 'If you take them at once.'

27 'shpry': spry (moved at speed).

'Then the fun began. Shmall weemin is more up in themselves than big wans. So the shtage managers an' bally masters what was in the habit of drillin' childher in the pantomime sayson soon found out the differ.[28] Some iv them thried to thrate[29] the little weemin - "beautiful childher" is what I called them, so they thought I was a very nice man, an' we got on well with aich other, an' I had no quarrellin' wid them - as if they was kids, an' ordhered them about somethin' crool. They soon found out the mishtake. Wan iv them - Cuthbert Kinsey it was, of the Royal at Queenhythe[30] - gave wan iv them[31] a slap on th' ear. But she could scrap a bit, so she could; she was a sturdy, plucky little party what could whip her weight in wild cats, as the Yankees say. She just put up her dooks[32] an' wint for him. She gave him wan on the bread-basket an' another on the boko what made him go into the claret business sthraight.[33] So for that sayson he kep his hooks down. My! but there was scrappin' in some theyatres, for the budlets wouldn't shtand no guff. An' whin the bally masters an' shtage managers found they was weemin an' tried to make love to them things was worse. Moreover, they tuk breaches iv promise whiniver the chap had any oof[34] at all. I'm tellin' ye the carnage among bachelors in theyatres that year was frightful. I was a bachelor meself in thim days, so I have cause enough to know it!'

'Was that when and how you met your wife, Mr Roscoe?'[35] asked the Second Old Woman, a big-built woman with a temper of her own.

The rest of the Company smiled, for it was an open secret that Mrs Roscoe, who had once been wardrobe mistress, had been

---

28 'Stage managers and ballet masters ... found out the difference.'

29 'thrate': threaten.

30 Once a famous East End theatre beside Southwark Bridge, London.

31 'wan iv them': one of them.

32 'dooks': dukes. Cockney rhyming slang for 'Duke of York's'; which rhymes with 'porks', which means 'fists'.

33 'She gave him a blow to the stomach and a second to the 'boko' (nose) that made it bleed - 'into the claret business straight'.

34 The term is 'got his hoof (foot) in', which means that the man sought a permanent relationship leading to marriage. Should he renege on his engagement, it used to be the case under English law that the jilted woman could sue him for 'breach of promise'.

35 Mr Roscoe? The Super-Master's name is given as Murphy.

required to leave the Company on account of her success in a face-slapping episode wherein the Second Old Woman had fared badly. The Super Master, who, both as one occupying a post on the managerial staff and also as an Irishman from whom a large measure of courtesy to women was expected, kept strict guard on his temper except when quelling a riot or pleasantry amongst his own crowd, answered sweetly:

'Yes, ma'am. I am proud to say it was. I bless the day.'

'She is not here, I notice,' said the Second Old Woman, with a suavity equal to his own. 'May I ask you why that is?'

'Certainly, ma'am,' he replied heartily. 'She is away on a long tour in America with a first-class Company.'

'Oh! And she is Wardrobe – as an assistant, I suppose?'

'No, ma'am,' he replied sadly. 'I regret to say she has gone down in the world.'

'I see. A Dresser,[36] then?'

'No, ma'am. Lower still; she is First Old Woman. But then I should say that it is a Company so good that the Old Women are played by young and pretty ones. Not by real has-beens or never-wases, as is usually the case!' The ready laugh of the younger members of the Company showed that the shot had told. The Second Old Woman's anger flamed out in her face as she said still – by a great effort – suavely:

'I hope she is now respectable?'

'Keeps, ma'am! – keeps, not "is"! She is and has always been respectable. And is always a quiet, tender-hearted woman. Except, of course, when she has to chastise insolence – as you very well know.'

The Second Old Woman contented herself by glaring, as she realised from the universal titter that the laugh was against her. The Super Master swallowed his consolation – steaming hot though it was.

The MC turned to the next on the line, The Advance Agent,[37] an alert-looking man of middle age.

---

36 A Dresser is the personal assistant to a leading performer.

37 Advance publicity. The Agent was personally responsible for getting the best publicity before the company set foot in town. This is obviously the end of the season or he would not be with the others on the train. Nowadays he would do this work by phone.

'I hope you will give us something next, Alphage. It is so seldom that we have the honour of seeing you whilst we are on the road that we should look on it as the lost opportunity of our lives if we do not hear some story or reminiscence of your own life.'

'All right, old man. I'll do what I can. You won't mind, I hope, Ladies and Gentlemen, if it is a bit dull. But the fact is that I've been so much in the habit of inventing lies about my stars that plain fact comes to be prosaic. Anyhow, it may be a change for me; I'm tired of finding out new virtues of my employers or ringing the changes on the old ones.

13

A Criminal Star

'OF course, you all remember Wolseley Gartside –'

'Rather!' This was from the Tragedian. 'I remember when he took that name. Indeed, I was not pleased with him about it; it clashed with the name I had taken myself – or, rather – ahem! – which my sponsors took for me at my christening. I consoled myself with the reflection that Wolseley was a later name historically than Wellesley.' The Advance Agent went on:

'Gartside, like many others who have risen from the ranks – the ranks of his profession – was, well, a wee, tiny bit over-sensitive in matters of public esteem. In fact, he did not like to be neglected –'

Here the Second Heavies interrupted with a rapidity and acerbity which left an impression that indignation was founded on aggrievement:

'"Over-sensitive in matters of public esteem!" I like that. He had got the swelled head bad, if that be what you mean. He wanted the earth, he did! The way he hustled other people off the posters was indecent! And the size of type he clamoured for was an inducement to blindness and an affront to the common sense of an educated community.'[1] The Advance Agent went on calmly:

'– did not like to be neglected. This was all bad enough when he was engaged by someone else; but when he was out on his own with nothing to check him except the reports of his treasurer,[2] he became a holy terror. There wasn't any crowding of names off the bill then; there were simply no names at all. Names of other people, I mean; his name was all right so long as the paper was up to the biggest stands, and the types were the largest to be had in the town. Later on he went even further and had all his printing done in

---

1 Most actors worry more about their 'billing' than their performance. But they would swear it is their agent who is making all the fuss.

2 'treasurer': the Manager on tour.

London or New York from types cut special.' The Second Heavies cut in again:

'No! Mr Wolseley Gartside didn't mean to get neglected so long as there was a public Press to be influenced or a hoarding to be covered.'

'Exactly!' said the Advance Agent drily. He was beginning to fear that his pitch would be queered by the outpouring of the grievances of the Second Heavies. The professional instinct of the audience made for peace. They were all trained to listen. Mr Alphage seized the opportunity, and went on:

'When he was arranging his first American tour he wanted to get someone who, as a *persona grata*,[3] could command the Press; who understood human nature to the core; who had the instinct of a diplomatist, the experience of a field-marshall, the tact of an Attorney-General; the –'

'All right, old man. We know you took him in tow.'

'Thank you, Bones! I understand. Gartside was a tragedian, too, and of course wanted the whole stage. They're all the same.'

'Well, of all the –' began Dovercourt; but there he stopped. There was a readiness of repartee about the Advance Agent that disturbed his self-serenity.

'So I took him in tow, as Bones calls it. I thought my work was piloting.[4] But Bones knows; he, too, belongs to the hungry, egotist lot who have to be dragged into publicity – like Wolseley Gartside!

'Well, before I started out, which he insisted should be a full week ahead of him, he began to teach me my business. At first I pointed out to him that the whole mechanism of advance publicity wasn't wrong because he hadn't done it. But he took me up short, and expressed his opinions pretty freely, I admit. He gave me quite a dissertation on publicity, telling me that to hit the public you must tell them plenty. They wanted to know all about a man; they didn't care much whether it was good or bad; but on the whole they preferred bad. Then he went on to give me what he called my

---

3 A favoured person.

4 When the 'pilot' is on board a ship, even the captain stands to one side.

instructions. That I was to have paragraphs about him every day. "Make me out," he said, "a sort of Don Juan, with a fierce, revengeful nature. A man from whose hate no man is safe; no woman from his love. Never mind moral character. The public don't want it – nor no more do I. Say whatever you please about me so long as you make people talk. Now I don't want argument with you. Do you just carry out my instructions, and all will be well. But if you don't, you'll get the order of the chuck." I didn't want to argue with him. To begin with, a man like that isn't worth argument – especially about instructions. Instructions! Just fancy an Advance Agent who knows his business being *instructed* by a Star that he has got to boom, and to whose vanity – no, *sensitiveness* – he has to minister. Why, compared with even a duffer at my work the biggest and brightest star in the theatrical firmament don't know enough to come in out of the rain! I was very angry with him, I admit; but in a flash there came to me out of his own very instructions an idea which put anger out of my mind. The top dog isn't angry – though he may bite! "Very well, Mr Wolseley Gartside," said I to myself, said I, "I'll carry out your instructions with exactness. They're yours, not mine; so if anything comes out wrong you are the responsible party." Before I went to bed I wrote out a mem of my "instructions."

'"The public want to know everything about a man. Tell them plenty – all they want. They don't care whether it's good or bad. On the whole, they prefer bad. Give them paragraphs every day. Make me a Don Juan, fierce, revengeful, passionate. No man safe from my hate; no woman from my love. Don't aim at moral character; the public don't want it; no more do I. Say whatever you please about me so long as you make people talk. Make things lively before I come!"

'I headed this "Instructions to Montague Phase Alphage, Advance Agent to Wolseley Gartside, Esquire." In the morning I brought it to him and asked him to sign and date it, as I wished to carry out his instructions to the full, and to take for myself advantage of his wisdom and his splendid initiative power. He signed it, looking very pleased. The sort of smirk that tragedians use when they're feeling good.

'The next day I started out on my travels. The tour was to begin with a week of one-night stands. Wolseley Gartside had insisted on making out the tour himself, and, of course, he knew better than anybody - everybody else. You know what that means, Wragge. I certainly covered the ground for him that week. I simply lived in trains, and I wore out the stairs of all the offices of what they called newspapers. Do you know, I think there must be a special angelic squad told off to look after advance agents. And if there is, my chap must have had what they call a hellova time. It's a direct mercy that I didn't develop acute DT[5] in letting the penny-a-liners[6] of that group of one-horse towns have the time of their lives. They tumbled to it quick that they would not have to write any themselves, for, of course, I did all that myself. It was best that way, anyhow, for not one of them could have written a decent par[7] to save his soul.

'I filled them all up with Wolseley Gartside; and they filled up as much space as the editorial staff could spare from ads. Generally I paid for the printing, too - though who benefited by it I don't know. I thought Gartside would darken the air when he got my bill; but I did him well - in quantity, at all events. But the quality was good, too; just what the old man liked. I not only painted him as a man of transcendent genius and as an artist that had no peer in past or present, but gave him such a character as a libertine that the local Don Juans began over their drink to talk of reviving lynching, and the womenkind exhausted the dry goods stores for new frocks and fal-lals of all kinds. Why, they tell me that the demand for toupées and false fronts[8] and extensions was such that the New York wholesale hair houses sent down a whole flock of drummers. The back-numbers were going to have a turn at him as well as the girls and the frisky matrons! I gave him out as having the courage of a lion and the heart of a fiend; the skill at cards of a prestidigitateur;[9] the style and daring in the hunt of Buffalo Bill;[10] the learning of an Erasmus;[11] the voice of a De Reske;[12] the strength of Milo

---

5 'DT': Delirium tremens, no doubt from too much alcohol.

6 The basic rate of pay for a line of written copy.

7 Paragraph.

8 General hair-pieces to make the best of oneself.

9 An adept at sleight of hand.

10 'Buffalo Bill' Cody. Famous Indian fighter and hunter who became equally famous with his Wild West Show in the USA and Europe.

11 The Dutch Humanist and Historian of the 15th century.

12 Charles de Reske. The 19th-century concert singer who gave his name to the cigarette.

– it was before Sandow's time.[13] I finished it all off with a hypnotic gift which was unique; which from the stage could rule audiences, and in the smoking-room or the boudoir could make man or woman his obedient slave. I got most of the newspapers to take up hypnotism as a theme of controversy, and wrote lots of letters on the subject, under various names, which opened people's eyes as to the power of that mysterious craft – or quality, whichever it is – and the consequent danger attendant on their daily lives. I suppose I needn't say that the whole controversy everywhere circled round Gartside and his wonderful powers. I tell you that by the Sunday afternoon when my Star came along with his crowd in his special, with his private car at the tail of it,[14] and him on the rear platform, the women of Patricia City,[15] where he opened, were in a flutter. They didn't know whether it was hope or fear. Knowing the sex as I do, I am inclined to think it was hope. To tame and subdue a dragon of voluptuous impurity is the dearest wish of a good woman's heart!'

'Oh, really, Mr Phase Alphage ...' said the First Old Woman, raising an index finger of remonstrance.

'True, dear lady, true. It is trite as a record, as well as solemn as a truth.'

'Aye, it is truth, indeed. Sad truth!' murmured the Tragedian, in a thunderous bass. 'The experiences of my own hot youth have proven it to the full. 'Twas not gifts of mind or body, all-compelling though these be, nor the fascinations of our glamorous calling. Rather would I call it the maëlstrom of passion which the Apple of Eden begot in the breast of woman.'

'Rather a mixed metaphor that!' said the young man from Oxford, who seemed to have taken on himself the task of keeping the Tragedian to order. 'But we understand what you mean. Drive on, Alphage.'

'I was fifty miles on my road when the day of opening came; but

---

13 Milo and Sandow were famous strongmen in variety.

14 An entire 'special' train had been hired by the actor.

15 This name appears to be invention on Stoker's part.

I ran back – that came out of my own pocket, too! – to see Gartside and hear what he thought of the way I had exploited him. I boarded his train down the line, and came on with him. He was both jubilant and effusive, and said my work in advance was the best he had ever had. "Go on, my boy, go on, and follow it up. You are on the right tack!" were the last words he said to me. I dropped off at the depôt,[16] and got on the outward train, for I didn't want to get pitched into by him when he should find the excitement was less than he expected. I do believe he thought there would be in waiting a murderous crowd, with a rope, intent on a neck-tie party,[17] with a few regiments of State troops to counteract them.

'When I got into the next town the Press was full of what had been said at Patricia City, and wanted me to go at least one better, or they couldn't use my stuff at all. That would be checkmate to me as Advance Agent, so I was in a real difficulty. I couldn't increase the praise of my Star, so the only thing was to go down. I made up my mind to go deeper and deeper into crime. There was no help for it. I knew well that each other town in that group would want its own increase of pressure, and so arranged my plans in the back of my head. I should have to distribute the steps of the downward grade amongst five different towns; so I laid out my work and began to get my copy ready. I never went to bed at all that night, but spent it writing advance matter in shorthand. In the morning I got a smart typewriter and dictated to her from my stenographic script. I sent off that for Tuesday by mail, and got the rest ready to post when the hour should arrive. I had to be careful not to send matter long enough in advance for the comparison of towns, or of different papers in the same town.

'Early on Tuesday morning I got to Hustleville[18] – that was the second town of the tour – and from that moment matters began to hum. All the papers were full, not only of my own matter, but of comments on it. In addition, nearly every one had a leader[19] in

---

[16] This is not necessarily a passenger stop. It could be a stores area and place to take on water for the engine.

[17] A hanging; a lynch mob.

[18] Another invented name on Stoker's part.

[19] 'leader': a leading article, either by the paper's editor or an anonymous distinguished journalist, sometimes on the front page, sometimes not.

which they cut the Tragedian to pieces. *The Banner of Freedom* wanted to make out his coming to be nothing short of an international outrage.

'"It makes little," it said, "for the comity of nations that an ostensibly friendly country like England should be allowed to dump down on our shores a cargo of criminal decadents like the man Wolseley Gartside and his crowd of hooligans. His being left at large so long as seems to have been the case says little for either the morals or the sanity of the people who have permitted his existence. He is a smirch on the fair face of cosmic law, a living germ of intellectual disease, a cancerous growth even in the parasitic calling which he follows; an outrage to man and morals, to fair living, to development of God's creatures – nay, even to God Himself! The people of this State have not in the past lacked courage or energy to terminate swiftly, by the exercise of rough justice in the open courts of natural law, the opportunities of offenders against public good. We have heard of a human pendulum swinging on a giant bough of one of our noble forest trees; there are recollections in the minds of those of our pioneers who happily survive of worthless miscreants riding on rails clad in unpretentious costumes of feathers and tar. It is up to the heroic souls who founded Hustleville to break the long silence of their well-won repose, and, for protection of the city they have won from forest depths, and for the defence of their kin, to raise voice and hand for woman's honour and man's unshrinking nobility! A hint on such a subject should be sufficient. *Verbum sapientiœ sufficit.*[20] We have done."

'This reached Gartside after breakfast, and he at once wired me:

'"Go on; it is well. *Banner* has struck right note. Shall be ere long living heart of international cyclone!"

'I went on the same afternoon to Comstock, which was next on our route. I had, of course, sent on plenty of advance matter, and the editors had written me gratefully about it. But when I called at the *Whoop* – which was, I understood, the popular paper – I was received in a manner which was decidedly chilly. I am not, as a rule, lacking in diffidence ...'

---

20 'A word to the wise'.

'Distinctly an understatement, my dear sir,' said the Tragedian, with challenge to battle in his eye. You really wrong yourself by putting it in that negative way!' He glared in return, but went on, calmly:

'... but I admit I was a little nonplussed – no pun intended,[21] Governor' – this to the Manager. 'So I asked the editor if I had hurt or affronted him in any way to cause his greeting to be so different from his written words. He hum'd and haw'd, and finally admitted that he was chagrined that the Comstock *Whoop* had not been treated as well as the Hustleville *Banner of Freedom*.

'"How?" I asked. "I sent you twenty per cent more advance copy."[22]

'"Aye. The quantity was all right; but there were none of the spicy details which worked up the dormant conscience of even a one-horse town like Hustleville. Now, I suppose you know that we young towns can't live on the past. Has-been isn't a good diet for growing youth. Moreover, we're all living on one another's backs, with the nails dug in. What we want in the *Whoop* is anti-soothing syrup; and nothing else is any use to us. So get a move on you and let us have it. We want stronger meat than Hustleville."

'"But there's nothing stronger. To say more wouldn't be true."

'The editor seemed as if struck blind. He raised his hands as if expostulating with the powers of the air, as he said:

'"True! Do I live to hear the Advance Agent of a Troupe speak of truth ... Now, look here, Mister. It's no use talking ethics with you. For either I'm drunk – which would be early in the day for me – or else you've got some sort of freshness[23] on you that I don't understand. And I may tell you for your edification that we don't much care for freshness here. Comstock is a town where we perspire quick; and there's plenty of space in the forest for developing our cem-e-tary. When I got your first letter I told my boys to hold back because this was your funeral, and ye was up in the etiquette. But the boys wasn't altogether pleased. They are good

[21] Despite the disclaimer, this might be a pun, as the Actor Manager's name is Benville Nonplusser.

[22] 'advance copy': information about the play for use in the local paper.

[23] In this instance, cheekiness.

boys, and could knock sparks out of Ananias[24] in making a story. See! So you'd better get to work. You know your man and they don't; so your story is apt to seem more lifelike. I'll want the copy here by seven. Then, the quicker ye quit the better."

'There was nothing for it but to carry out Wolseley Gartside's *instructions*. It was wife-beating this time that swelled his reputation. I didn't mean to be knocked out by the boys of the *Whoop*, nor to afford an opportunity for exemplifying the sudorific[25] rapidity of Comstock - no, nor to take a part in de-veloping the cem-e-tary either; so the story of WG's experiences as a defendant in the police-court of Abingchester,[26] in the Peak of Derbyshire - that was well out of the way of public prints - was given in full detail, together with a description of the Lord Chancellor who condemned him, and an exciting account of his escape, riddled with bullets, from the county gaol.[27] The editor read it with a beaming face, and said when he had done:

'"That's the biggest scoop we ever had. Here, I'll give you a straight tip which will put money in your pocket if you get out your copy right smart. There is every indication that when the play is over to-morrow night there will be an adjournment of citizens to the forest, and that one of the oaks will bear a new sort of acorn. One with a bloated body; but a rotten heart. See?"

'I did see; and I sent an urgent letter to WG by the driver of the mail train, telling him frankly where his *instructions* were likely to lead him.

'He was wise for once, and altered his route. This wasn't a case for vanity, but for skin. So there wasn't any new kind of acorn found on the forest round Comstock, though the search party was all ready.

'Now, Mr Hempitch,' said the MC, 'you're next.' So he began at once.

'All right, sir. Mr Alphage's story of a Star reminds me of a Star of another kind which is more in my line of business.

---

24 Ananias was struck dead by God for lying to St Peter. See Acts 5.

25 To cause sweating.

26 There is no such English town.

27 The idea of a shoot-out in a Derbyshire gaol is ludicrous. Sounds more like the OK Corral.

14

A Star Trap

'When I was apprenticed to theatrical carpentering my master was John Haliday, who was Master Machinist – we called men in his post "Master Carpenter" in those days – of the old Victoria Theatre, Hulme.[1] It wasn't called Hulme; but that name will do. It would only stir up painful memories if I were to give the real name. I daresay some of you – not the Ladies (this with a gallant bow all round) – will remember the case of a Harlequin[2] as was killed in an accident in the pantomime. We needn't mention names; Mortimer will do for a name to call him by – Henry Mortimer. The cause of it was never found out. But I knew it; and I've kept silence for so long that I may speak now without hurting anyone. They're all dead long ago that was interested in the death of Henry Mortimer or the man who wrought that death.

'Any of you who know of the case will remember what a handsome, dapper, well-built man Mortimer was. To my own mind he was the handsomest man I ever saw.'

The Tragedian's low, grumbling whisper, 'That's a large order,' sounded a warning note. Hempitch, however, did not seem to hear it, but went on:

'Of course, I was only a boy then, and I hadn't seen any of you gentlemen – Yer very good health, Mr Wellesley Dovercourt, sir, and cettera. I needn't tell you, Ladies, how well a harlequin's dress[3] sets off a nice slim figure. No wonder that in these days of suffragettes,[4] women wants to be harlequins as well as columbines.[5]

---

1 The 'Hippodrome', Hulme, Manchester, continued as a good 'number two' tour date right up to the 1960s.

2 Some traditional Pantomimes retain a 'Harlequinade' sequence within the Christmas entertainment.

3 Tights in domino diamond patterns, and small black mask.

4 A political movement designed to protest for woman's equal rights.

5 A female dancer in a Pantomime; a sweetheart of Harlequin.

Though I hope they won't make the columbine a man's part!

'Mortimer was the nimblest chap at the traps I ever see. He was so sure of hisself that he would have extra weight put on so that when the counter weights fell he'd shoot up five or six feet higher than anyone else could even try to. Moreover, he had a way of drawing up his legs when in the air – the way a frog does when he is swimming – that made his jump look ever so much higher.

'I think the girls were all in love with him, the way they used to stand in the wings when the time was comin' for his entrance. That wouldn't have mattered much, for girls are always falling in love with some man or other, but it made trouble, as it always does when the married ones take the same start. There were several of these that were always after him, more shame for them, with husbands of their own. That was dangerous enough, and hard to stand for a man who might mean to be decent in any way. But the real trial – and the real trouble, too – was none other than the young wife of my own master, and she was more than flesh and blood could stand. She had come into the panto the season before as a high-kicker[6] – and she could! She could kick higher than girls that was more than a foot taller than her; for she was a wee bit of a thing and as pretty as pie; a gold-haired, blue-eyed, slim thing with much the figure of a boy, except for ...[7] and they saved her from any mistaken idea of that kind. Jack Haliday went crazy over her, and when the notice was up, and there was no young spark with plenty of oof[8] coming along to do the proper thing by her, she married him. It was, when they was joined, what you Ladies call a marriage of convenience; but after a bit they two got on very well, and we all thought she was beginning to like the old man – for Jack was old enough to be her father, with a bit to spare. In the summer, when the house was closed, he took her to the Isle of Man; and when they came back he made no secret of it that he'd had the happiest time of his life. She looked quite happy, too, and treated him affectionate; and we all began to think that *that* marriage had not been a failure at any rate.

---

6 'high-kickers' refers to the chorus line, not ballet. Theirs is a continuing tradition. They are popularly known as 'hoofers'.

7 One did not say 'breasts' or 'bosoms' in mixed company at the turn of the 20th century.

8 'oof': money, wealth.

'Things began to change, however, when the panto rehearsals began next year. Old Jack began to look unhappy, and didn't take no interest in his work. Loo - that was Mrs Haliday's name - didn't seem over fond of him now, and was generally impatient when he was by. Nobody said anything about this, however, to us men; but the married women smiled and nodded their heads and whispered that perhaps there were reasons. One day on the stage, when the harlequinade rehearsal was beginning, someone mentioned as how perhaps Mrs Haliday wouldn't be dancing that year, and they smiled as if they was all in the secret. Then Mrs Jack ups and gives them Johnny-up-the-orchard[9] for not minding their own business and telling a pack of lies, and such like as you Ladies like to express in your own ways when you get your back hair down.[10] The rest of us tried to soothe her all we could, and she went off home.

'It wasn't long after that that she and Henry Mortimer left together after rehearsal was over, he saying he'd leave her at home. She didn't make no objections - I told you he was a very handsome man.

'Well, from that on she never seemed to take her eyes from him during every rehearsal, right up to the night of the last rehearsal, which, of course, was full dress - "Everybody and Everything."[11]

'Jack Haliday never seemed to notice anything that was going on, like the rest of them did. True, his time was taken up with his own work, for I'm telling you that a Master Machinist hasn't got no loose time on his hands at the first dress rehearsal of a panto. And, of course, none of the company ever said a word or gave a look that would call his attention to it. Men and women are queer beings. They will be blind and deaf whilst danger is being run; and it's only after the scandal is beyond repair that they begin to talk - just the very time when most of all they should be silent.

'I saw all that went on, but I didn't understand it. I liked Mortimer myself and admired him - like I did Mrs Haliday, too - and I thought he was a very fine fellow. I was only a boy, you know, and Haliday's apprentice, so naturally I wasn't looking for any

9 Metaphorically, took a stick to them and chased them off.

10 'Free your hair' in readiness to defend yourselves.

11 Full costume, full make-up, and full scenery.

trouble I could help, even if I'd seen it coming. It was when I looked back afterwards at the whole thing that I began to comprehend; so you will all understand now, I hope, that what I tell you is the result of much knowledge of what I saw and heard and was told of afterwards – all morticed and clamped up by thinking.

'The panto had been on about three weeks when one Saturday, between the shows, I heard two of our company talking. Both of them was among the extra girls that both sang and danced and had to make theirselves useful. I don't think either of them was better than she should be;[12] they went out to too many champagne suppers with young men that had money to burn. That part doesn't matter in this affair – except that they was naturally enough jealous of women who was married – which was what they was aiming at – and what lived straighter than they did. Women of that kind like to see a good woman tumble down; it seems to make them all more even. Now real bad girls what have gone under altogether will try to save a decent one from following their road. That is, so long as they're young; for a bad one what is long in the tooth[13] is the limit. They'll help anyone down hill – so long as they get anything out of it.

'Well – no offence, you Ladies, as has growed up! – these two girls was enjoyin' themselves over Mrs Haliday and the mash[14] she had set up on Mortimer. They didn't see that I was sitting on a stage box behind a built-out piece of the Prologue of the panto, which was set ready for night. They were both in love with Mortimer, who wouldn't look at either of them, so they was miaw'n cruel, like cats on the tiles. Says one:

'"The Old Man seems worse than blind; he *won't* see."

'"Don't you be too sure of that," says the other. "He don't mean to take no chances. I think you must be blind, too, Kissie." That was her name – on the bills anyhow, Kissie Mountpelier. "Don't he make a point of taking her home hisself every night after the play. You should know, for you're in the hall yourself waiting for your young man till he comes from his club."

---

12 This refers to loose morals.

13 The shrinkage of the gums with advancing age makes the teeth appear longer.

14 'mash': flirtation.

'"Wot-ho, you bally geeser,"[15] says the other – which her language was mostly coarse – "don't you know there's two ends to everything? The Old Man looks to one end only!" Then they began to snigger and whisper; and presently the other one says:

'"Then he thinks harm can be only done when work is over!"

'"Jest so," she answers. "Her and him knows that the old man has to be down long before the risin' of the rag;[16] but she doesn't come in till the Vision of Venus dance after half time; and he not till the harlequinade!"

Then I quit. I didn't want to hear any more of that sort.

'All that week things went on as usual. Poor old Haliday wasn't well. He looked worried and had a devil of a temper. I had reason to know that, for what worried him was his work. He was always a hard worker, and the panto season was a terror with him. He didn't ever seem to mind anything else outside his work. I thought at the time that that was how those two chattering girls made up their slanderous story; for, after all, a slander, no matter how false it may be, must have some sort of beginning. Something that seems, if there isn't something that is! But no matter how busy he might be, old Jack always made time to leave the wife at home.

'As the week went on he got more and more pale; and I began to think he was in for some sickness. He generally remained in the theatre between the shows on Saturday;[17] that is, he didn't go home, but took a high tea[18] in the coffee shop close to the theatre, so as to be handy in case there might be a hitch anywhere in the preparation for night. On that Saturday he went out as usual when the first scene was set, and the men were getting ready the packs[19] for the rest of the scenes. By and bye there was some trouble – the usual Saturday kind[20] – and I went off to tell him. When I went into the coffee shop I couldn't see him. I thought it best not to ask or to seem to take any notice, so I came back to the theatre, and

15 Here, 'bally' equates with randy, though usually it acts as an expletive.

16 The raising of the main curtain to reveal the stage.

17 At that time there would usually be no afternoon matinee on Saturdays, in view of weekend shopping, but a First and Second House, commencing at 6.30pm and 8.30pm.

18 'high tea': a light cooked course taken at tea-time in Scotland and the north of England.

19 To correctly stack the scenery ready for quick-change scenes.

20 The men have been paid, so they have been drinking.

heard that the trouble had settled itself as usual, by the men who had been quarrelling going off to have another drink. I hustled up those who remained, and we got things smoothed out in time for them all to have their tea. Then I had my own. I was just then beginning to feel the responsibility of my business, so I wasn't long over my food, but came back to look things over and see that all was right, especially the trap, for that was a thing Jack Haliday was most particular about. He would overlook a fault for anything else; but if it was along of a trap, the man had to go. He always told the men that that wasn't ordinary work; it was life or death.[21]

'I had just got through my inspection when I saw old Jack coming in from the hall. There was no one about at that hour, and the stage was dark. But dark as it was I could see that the old man was ghastly pale. I didn't speak, for I wasn't near enough, and as he was moving very silently behind the scenes I thought that perhaps he wouldn't like anyone to notice that he had been away. I thought the best thing I could do would be to clear out of the way, so I went back and had another cup of tea.

'I came away a little before the men, who had nothing to think of except to be in their places when Haliday's whistle sounded. I went to report myself to my master, who was in his own little glass-partitioned den at the back of the carpenter's shop. He was there bent over his own bench, and was filing away at something so intently that he did not seem to hear me; so I cleared out. I tell you, Ladies and Gents, that from an apprentice point of view it is not wise to be too obtrusive when your master is attending to some private matter of his own!

'When the "get-ready" time came and the lights went up, there was Haliday as usual at his post. He looked very white and ill – so ill that the stage manager, when he came in, said to him that if he liked to go home and rest he would see that all his work would be

---

21 A star trap is an opening in the stage which propels an actor upwards through the floor at great speed. Each segment is triangular, the points of the star meeting in the middle. The wedges are hinged to the circumference, which enables them to fly upwards as the body is catapulted through the trap. The wedges fall back in place so quickly that the audience cannot see what has happened, the actor materialising as if by magic. The star trap was so dangerous it was eventually banned. If the pieces of the star failed to open and close properly, a performer could jump short and be impaled round the waist.

attended to. He thanked him, and said that he thought he would be able to stay. "I do feel a little weak and ill, sir," he said. "I felt just now for a few moments as if I was going to faint. But that's gone by already, and I'm sure I shall be able to get through the work before us all right."

'Then the doors was opened, and the Saturday night audience came rushing and tumbling in. The Victoria was a great Saturday night house. No matter what other nights might be, *that* was sure to be good. They used to say in the perfesh[22] that the Victoria lived on it, and that the management was on holiday for the rest of the week. The actors knew it, and no matter how slack they might be from Monday to Friday they was all taut and trim then. There was no walking through and no fluffing on Saturday nights – or else they'd have had the bird.[23]

'Mortimer was one of the most particular of the lot in this way. He never was slack at any time – indeed, slackness is not a harlequin's fault, for if there's slackness there's no harlequin, that's all. But Mortimer always put on an extra bit on the Saturday night. When he jumped up through the star trap he always went then a couple of feet higher. To do this we had always to put on a lot more weight. This he always saw to himself; for, mind you, it's no joke being driven up through the trap as if you was shot out of a gun. The points of the star had to be kept free, and the hinges at their bases must be well oiled, or else there can be a disaster at any time. Moreover, 'tis the duty of someone appointed for the purpose to see that all is clear upon the stage. I remember hearing that once at New York, many years ago now, a harlequin was killed by a "grip" – as the Yankees call a carpenter – what outsiders here call a scene-shifter – walking over the trap just as the stroke had been given to let go the counter-weights. It wasn't much satisfaction to the widow to know that the "grip" was killed too.[24]

'That night Mrs Haliday looked prettier than ever, and kicked even higher than I had ever seen her do. Then, when she got

---

22 'perfesh': theatrical profession.

23 'had the bird': to be sacked, or 'given the bird' (booed) by the audience.

24 Barry Lupino, of the famous family of acrobats and clowns, and himself a great Pantomime Dame, always attended to the star trap himself. He insisted it was only dangerous to amateurs.

dressed for home, she came as usual and stood in the wings for the beginning of the harlequinade. Old Jack came across the stage and stood beside her; I saw him from the back follow up the sliding ground-row[25] that closed in on the Realms of Delight. I couldn't help noticing that he still looked ghastly pale. He kept turning his eyes on the star trap. Seeing this, I naturally looked at it too, for I feared lest something might have gone wrong. I had seen that it was in good order, and that the joints were properly oiled when the stage was set for the evening show, and as it wasn't used all night for anything else I was reassured. Indeed, I thought I could see it shine a bit as the limelight caught the brass hinges. There was a spot light just above it on the bridge, which was intended to make a good show of harlequin and his big jump. The people used to howl with delight as he came rushing up through the trap and when in the air drew up his legs and spread them wide for an instant and then straightened them again as he came down – only bending his knees just as he touched the stage.

'When the signal was given the counter-weight worked properly. I knew, for the sound of it at that part was all right.

'But something was wrong. The trap didn't work smooth, and open at once as the harlequin's head touched it. There was a shock and a tearing sound, and the pieces of the star seemed torn about, and some of them were thrown about the stage. And in the middle of them came the coloured and spangled figure that we knew.

'But somehow it didn't come up in the usual way. It was erect enough, but there was not the usual elasticity. The legs never moved; and when it went up a fair height – though nothing like usual – it seemed to topple over and fall on the stage on its side. The audience shrieked, and the people in the wings – actors and staff all the same – closed in, some of them in their stage clothes, others dressed for going home. But the man in the spangles lay quite still.

'The loudest shriek of all was from Mrs Haliday; and she was the first to reach the spot where he – it – lay. Old Jack was close behind her, and caught her as she fell. I had just time to see that, for I

---

25 A low-cut piece of scenery, usually representing a coastline, or even waves, in a lake or seaside scene.

made it my business to look after the pieces of the trap; there was plenty of people to look after the corpse. And the pit[26] was by now crossing the orchestra and climbing up on the stage.

'I managed to get the bits together before the rush came. I noticed that there were deep scratches on some of them, but I didn't have time for more than a glance. I put a stage box over the hole lest anyone should put a foot through it. Such would mean a broken leg at least; and if one fell through, it might mean worse. Amongst other things I found a queer-looking piece of flat steel with some bent points on it. I knew it didn't belong to the trap; but it came from *somewhere*, so I put it in my pocket.

'By this time there was a crowd where Mortimer's body lay. That he was stone dead nobody could doubt. The very attitude was enough. He was all straggled about in queer positions; one of the legs was doubled under him with the toes sticking out in the wrong way. But let that suffice! It doesn't do to go into details of a dead body ... I wish someone would give me a drop of punch.

'There was another crowd round Mrs Haliday, who was lying a little on one side nearer the wings[27] where her husband had carried her and laid her down. She, too, looked like a corpse; for she was as white as one and as still, and looked as cold. Old Jack was kneeling beside her, chafing her hands. He was evidently frightened about her, for he, too, was deathly white. However, he kept his head, and called his men round him. He left his wife in care of Mrs Homcroft, the Wardrobe Mistress, who had by this time hurried down. She was a capable woman, and knew how to act promptly. She got one of the men to lift Mrs Haliday and carry her up to the wardrobe.[28] I heard afterwards that when she got her there she turned out all the rest of them that followed up – the women as well as the men – and looked after her herself.

'I put the pieces of the broken trap on the top of the stage box, and told one of our chaps to mind them, and see that no one

---

26 At the turn of the 20th century this was the cheap seating immediately behind the orchestra stalls under the circle overhang.

27 The sides of the stage masked from audience view.

28 The large room, generally either high up in the dressing room areas or right under the stage, set aside for maintenance of costumes. There, the wardrobe mistress is a power above all others.

touched them, as they might be wanted. By this time the police who had been on duty in front had come round, and as they had at once telephoned to headquarters, more police kept coming in all the time. One of them took charge of the place where the broken trap was; and when he heard who put the box and the broken pieces there sent for me. More of them took the body away to the property room, which was a large room with benches in it, and which could be locked up. Two of them stood at the door, and wouldn't let anyone go in without permission.

'The man who was in charge of the trap asked me if I had seen the accident. When I said I had, he asked me to describe it. I don't think he had much opinion of my powers of description, for he soon dropped that part of his questioning. Then he asked me to point out where I found the bits of the broken trap. I simply said:

'"Lord bless you, sir, I couldn't tell. They was scattered all over the place. I had to pick them up between people's feet as they were rushing in from all sides."

'"All right, my boy," he said, in quite a kindly way, for a policeman, "I don't think they'll want to worry you. There are lots of men and women, I am told, who were standing by and saw the whole thing. They will be all subpœnaed."[29] I was a small-made lad in those days – I ain't a giant now! – and I suppose he thought it was no use having children for witnesses when they had plenty of grown-ups. Then he said something about me and an idiot asylum that was not kind – no, nor wise either, for I dried up and did not say another word.

'Gradually the public was got rid of. Some strolled off by degrees, going off to have a glass before the pubs closed, and talk it all over. The rest of us and the police ballooned out. Then, when the police had taken charge of everything and put in men to stay all night, the coroner's officer came and took off the body to the city mortuary, where the police doctor made a post mortem. I was allowed to go home. I did so – and gladly – when I had seen the place settling down. Mr Haliday took his wife home in a four-wheeler.[30] It was

---

29 A Writ, commanding a person to appear in a court of justice.

30 Four-wheeled horse cab, as opposed to a cheaper and less comfortable Hansom, which seated only two. In a four-wheeler she would have been able to lie down.

perhaps just as well, for Mrs Homcroft and some other kindly souls had poured so much whisky and brandy and rum and gin and beer and peppermint into her that I don't believe she could have walked if she had tried.

'When I was undressing myself something scratched my leg as I was taking off my trousers. I found it was the piece of flat steel which I had picked up on the stage. It was in the shape of a star fish, but the spikes of it were short. Some of the points were turned down, the rest were pulled out straight again. I stood with it in my hand wondering where it had come from and what it was for, but I couldn't remember anything in the whole theatre that it could have belonged to. I looked at it closely again, and saw that the edges were all filed and quite bright. But that did not help me, so I put it on the table and thought I would take it with me in the morning; perhaps one of the chaps might know. I turned out the gas[31] and went to bed – and to sleep.

'I must have begun to dream at once, and it was, naturally enough, all about the terrible thing that occurred. But, like all dreams, it was a bit mixed. They were all mixed. Mortimer with his spangles flying up the trap, it breaking, and the pieces scattering round. Old Jack Haliday looking on at one side of the stage with his wife beside him – he as pale as death, and she looking prettier than ever. And then Mortimer coming down all crooked and falling on the stage. Mrs Haliday shrieking, and her and Jack running forward, and me picking up the pieces of the broken trap from between people's legs, and finding the steel star with the bent points.

'I woke in a cold sweat, saying to myself as I sat up in bed in the dark:

'"That's it!"'

'And then my head began to reel about so that I lay down again and began to think it all over. And it all seemed clear enough then. It was Mr Haliday who made that star and put it over the star trap where the points joined! That was what Jack Haliday was filing at when I saw him at his bench; and he had done it because Mortimer and his wife had been making love to each other. Those girls were right, after all. Of course, the steel points had prevented the trap

---

31 That is, gas lights.

opening, and when Mortimer was driven up against it his neck was broken.

'But then came the horrible thought that if Jack did it, it was murder, and he would be hung. And, after all, it was his wife that the harlequin had made love to – and old Jack loved her very much indeed himself and had been good to her – and she was his wife. And that bit of steel would hang him if it should be known. But no one but me – and whoever made it, and put it on the trap – even knew of its existence – and Mr Haliday was my master – and the man was dead – and he was a villain!

'I was living then at Quarry Place; and in the old quarry was a pond so deep that the boys used to say that far down the water was boiling hot, it was so near Hell.

'I softly opened the window, and, there in the dark, threw the bit of steel as far as I could into the quarry.

'No one ever knew, for I have never spoken a word of it till this very minute. I was not called at the inquest. Everyone was in a hurry; the coroner and the jury and the police. Our governor was in a hurry too, because we wanted to go on as usual at night; and too much talk of the tragedy would hurt business. So nothing was known; and all went on as usual. Except that after that Mrs Haliday didn't stand in the wings during the harlequinade, and she was as loving to her old husband as a woman can be. It was him she used to watch now; and always with a sort of respectful adoration. She knew, though no one else did, except her husband – and me.'

When he finished there was a big spell of silence. The company had all been listening intently, so that there was no change except the cessation of Hempitch's voice. The eyes of all were now fixed on Mr Wellesley Dovercourt. It was the *rôle* of the Tragedian to deal with such an occasion. He was quite alive to the privileges of his status, and spoke at once:

'H'm! Very excellent indeed! You will have to join the ranks of our profession, Mr Master Machinist – the lower ranks, of course. A very thrilling narrative yours, and distinctly true. There may be some errors of detail, such as that Mrs Haliday never flirted again. I ... I knew John Haliday under, of course, his real name. But I shall preserve the secret you so judiciously suppressed. A very worthy person. He was stage carpenter at the Duke's Theatre, Bolton,[32] where I first dared histrionic triumphs in the year - ah H'm! I saw quite a good deal of Mrs Haliday at that time. And you are wrong about her. Quite wrong! She was a most attractive little woman - very!'

The Wardrobe Mistress here whispered to the Second Old Woman:

'Well, ma'am, they all seem agoin' of it to-night. I think they must have ketched the infection from Mr Bloze. There isn't a bally word of truth in all Hempitch has said. I was there when the accident occurred - for it was an accident when Jim Bungnose, the clown, was killed. For he was a clown, not a 'arlequin; an' there wasn't no lovemakin' with Mrs 'Aliday. God 'elp the woman as would try to make love to Jim; which she was the Strong Woman in a Circus, and could put up her dooks like a man. Moreover, there wasn't no Mrs 'Aliday. The carpenter at Grimsby,[33] where it is he means, was Tom Elrington, as he was my first 'usband. And as to Mr Dovercourt rememberin''! He's a cure,[34] he is; an' the Limit!'

The effect of the Master Machinist's story was so depressing that the MC tried to hurry things on; any change of sentiment would, he thought, be an advantage. So he bustled along:

'Now, Mr Turner Smith, you are the next on the roster. It is a pity we have not an easel and a canvas and paint box here, or even some cartridge paper and charcoal, so that you might give us a touch of your art - what I may call a plastic diversion of the current of narrative genius which has been enlivening the snowy waste around us.' The artistic audience applauded this flight of metaphor - all except the young man from Oxford, who contented himself by saying loudly, 'Pip-pip!' He had heard something like it before at the Union.[35] The Scene Painter saw coming danger, for the Tragedian had put down his pipe and was clearing his throat; so he at once began:

---

32 A fictitious theatre in Bolton, Lancashire, in the north-west of England.

33 Grimsby is a fishing port on the east coast of England, on the River Humber.

34 He will offer a solution or cure, in this instance. Stoker seems to have forgotten that Ma admitted in 'Coggin's' Property' that she had never married. Either that, or she is now talking nonsense through drink.

35 The Oxford Union. The debating society of the university students.

15

A Moon-Light Effect

'I'M afraid I cannot give any narrative of a humorous or touching nature. My life has been, as is necessary for the art I follow, an unexciting one. Perhaps it has been just as well; for art requires a measure of calmness if not of isolation for its higher manifestations. Perfection was never achieved amid the silent tumult of conflicting thoughts.'

'Pip-pip' came again from the young man from Oxford. The Tragedian started to his feet – in his momentary passion he forgot to be slow.

'I protest against this unseemly interruption. This intrusion into the privacy of our artistic life of hooligans without soul: this importation to the inner heart of refinement, of the coarser vulgarisms of the world of decadent ineptitude. And when, in addition, the perpetrators of this ignoble infamy seem to be ignorant of the very elemental basis of the respect due to recognised personal supremacy in a glorious art and an honoured calling. Bah! Never mind, Turner Smith.[1] I suppose all the fine arts are to be assailed in turns. Your time will come, however. You can, later, turn this painful episode to professional advantage. I understand that you are doing the scenery of the panto at Poole;[2] why not take for the subject of your opening scene, the gloomy one, *The Home of the Hooligan.* The audience will show at once their detestation of that offensive class. Doubtless the Costumier will rise to the occasion, and show a peculiarly offensive fiend with a marvel of ill manners. The Musical Conductor, too, can enhance the satirical effect by introducing into his score as a *motif* the Pip-pip whereby the Hooligan proclaims himself.' Then the Tragedian retired into himself with a victorious air. In the

1 It is a custom in England (then and now) to baptise a child not only in the family name but in the name of one admired. JMW Turner, one of Britain's greatest ever artists, began as a scene-painter at Drury Lane.

2 Poole, Dorset, on the south coast of England.

constrained silence that followed the Wardrobe Mistress was heard to whisper to the Sewing Woman:

'Mister Wellesley Dovercourt giv it him in the neck that time. It'll be a lesson to Cattle what he won't forget.' Cattle was the nickname of the young man from Oxford, given to him soon after his joining the company. The occasion had been his writing his name in a landlady's 'book'[3] and putting after it, Oxon. This was looked on by his comrades not as cheek but as bad spelling. The Scene Painter[4] saw his chance to continue, and so resumed his narrative:

'I was Scenic Artist at one time to old Schoolbred, the impresario. It was a special engagement, and just suited me, for at that time I had undertaken a lot of work of various kinds, and was looking about for a painting room. Schoolbred had then a long lease of the Queen's Opera House,[5] which had, as some of you may remember, a magnificent *atelier.* Old Schoolbred paid me a good salary – that is, he *promised* it, for he never paid any one if he could help it. I daresay he suspected that I mistrusted him, for he also put it in the agreement that I was to have full use of the painting-room for my own purposes from the time of my signing until I should start at his work. It was then that my solicitor[6] did a wise thing. He, too, knew from old experience that there was sure to be some trouble with Schoolbred, and insisted that I should have a lease of the painting rooms. "Otherwise," he said, "your own property is not safe. If he goes bankrupt the creditors will seize all of yours that is on the premises." When I objected he said:

---

3 It is a police regulation that guests register in hotels, inns and boarding houses by giving their name and home address. 'Oxon' is a diminutive of Oxonian (an Oxford man), and has snobbish connotations.

4 A large company with an extensive repertoire of plays would travel with a Scenic Artist to keep all scenery in good order.

5 There is no longer a Queen's Opera House. It once stood on the site of the also demolished Stoll at the bottom of Kingsway (built by impresario Oswald Stoll) but was moved back to make room for the new tram underpass. The Queen's included its own painters' studio ('atelier'). It was a block away from Irving's Lyceum and may have been used by Stoker on Irving's behalf. There was also a Queen's Theatre on Long Acre, demolished in the 1870s.

6 'solicitor': a legal practitioner who advises clients and prepares cases but who is not empowered to advocate in higher courts.

'"Surely it is all the same to you. You will give him each week a quittance for salary, and he will give you one for rent. It is as broad as it is long; and you wouldn't touch money anyhow." As he found all materials and paid wages I was on velvet, for I should have no expenses. All I risked was my time; and against that I had the use of the finest frames[7] in London. Schoolbred's work was only touching up the old scenes belonging to the Opera House and painting the new opera by Magnoli, *Il Campador.* My assistant, whom he paid, could do most of the re-painting, and as I knew that his work did not come on till September I had nearly six months rent free, and my time my own.

'When I had moved in my traps[8] I got to work at once. It took me half a day going over the scenery book with Grimshaw, who was then the Stage Carpenter, and off and on a couple of days more examining the scenes before we could get to work. The scenery was old-fashioned – nearly all flats;[9] hardly a cloth, let alone a cut-cloth,[10] in the lot. Heavy old framed stuff that wouldn't fold; and as much messy old timber about it as would furnish a ship-yard. Old Schoolbred had ordered the scenes to be made workable, so that when the time should come of bringing the operas on the road[11] they should be all ready. There would, I saw, be a fine old job for Grimshaw to cut and hinge that mass of scenes so that they would double up[12] for transport. However, Grimshaw was a good man, and work was no terror to him. He got his coat off, and once he was started with his own men I couldn't overtake him. Schoolbred was in a hurry to have the work done – in such a hurry that he didn't even grumble when I had to get a second assistant and two more labourers. Mind you, that meant a lot to him, for weekly wages means ready money; and out-of-pocket expenses have to be paid every Saturday. There were seventeen operas, so that it was no slouch of a job to get them all into moving trim. But there is, I must

---

7 Painting frames that were vast enough to take a full-sized 'cloth'; a background for a scene on canvas that could be raised and lowered like a (drop) curtain.

8 In this instance, 'baggage'.

9 'flats': canvas stretched on wooden frames to be cleated (roped) together.

10 'cut-cloth': cloth cut at one side in the shape of trees, etc.

11 Not in the literal sense. Travel on tour between towns was by train.

12 Fold in half, face to face.

say, this about a carpenter's job that when the "production" is simplified it means saving labour afterwards. But the more scenes there are - not built scenes, but flats and cloths, wings and borders[13] - to keep in order for nightly use and travel, and the taking to and from the storage, the more the poor scenic artist gets it in the neck.

'However, when we had once got started and I had explained to my assistants what I wanted and roughed out sketches to guide them I was able to get a bit of my own work in hand. I had a whole batch of such at the time. As you know, it was just when I was starting on my own, and every scene that was done was just so much in my pocket. I tell you I worked hard to get a bit ahead and give myself room, so that I wouldn't have to be always pulling the devil by the tail.[14] We all worked day and night; as old Schoolbred didn't grumble at overtime the men were content to do twenty-four hours in the day. Our work has long waits; and as the labourers have to be on hand whenever they are wanted they did themselves well in the way of sleep. At first they had old sacks and such like to lie on; but presently they got luxurious, and nothing would do them but ticking and fresh hay[15] and army blankets to cover them. I didn't mind. Indeed, I never even let on that I noticed.

After all, the men had to rest *some time*, and when they slept in the theatre it saved them their lodging. As you know, we scenic artists sometimes have our food cooked for us in the paint room in busy times, so that these men lived pretty well free. Naturally, I charged all expenses, as old Schoolbred was in such a hurry that ordinary rules didn't count. He was glad to get the work done so quickly at any cost.

'I had on the frames then a set of scenes for *Manfred*,[16] which Wilbur Winston had commissioned. I had knocked off the other work quickly in order to be free for this. For this was a production that would make me. The scene of the *Thunderstorm in the Alps* would put me at the very top. That I held back, for I was anxious to

---

13 'wings' were for each side of the stage, 'borders' for overhead.

14 To tempt fate.

15 A strong material for mattress cases, filled with fresh hay. It was closely woven, against possible ticks.

16 Lord Byron's dramatic verse-drama set in the Alpine mountains.

make a great thing of it. It was my first job for Winston, and I wanted him to be pleased. Moreover, he had a great following, and a fine scene at the British[17] was talked about everywhere. There was a lot of built stuff in it and paperwork, so that by the time it was done it bulked up pretty big. It was still in hand when the opera season began. Winston wasn't ready for it, so he asked me to keep it till he should rehearse. Of course, I had to meet his wishes, but happily there was loads of room at the Queen's, even after we had arranged the operas separately so that we could deal with them as they came along. So there wasn't any trouble about that.

'At first the season seemed to promise well enough; but after a night or two business fell off, and Schoolbred was at his wits' end. He was already over head and ears in debt, and this time he was only given credit in the hope that those he owed to would get a bit back. They certainly treated him very well, I will say that. They gave him every possible chance; but when the creditors saw that so far from things getting better they were going from bad to worse, a meeting was held.

'At the meeting steps were taken, and very soon after Schoolbred was in process of being made a bankrupt. A Receiver was appointed by the Court, and took formal possession. Everyone in the theatre was upset about it – except me. I had my lease, and felt like a cock on his own dunghill.

'I found out, however, after a bit that it wasn't all sunshine even with a lease. As an employé I could get salary, if there was any to get; but the liquidator[18] cut down expenses, and, along with the rest, I was discharged. But as a lessor I was held to my lease and had to pay my rent. Long before this, as I said, old Schoolbred's work was finished, and I was working at my own contracts. I could not grumble much as my rent was small, and though I had had practically no salary in the past I had had the use of the *atelier.* So I paid up regularly, and was glad to be able to work. There was a little nuisance in one way; as the whole Opera house was in charge of the Receiver, and as my lease was only of a little bit of it I had to get a

---

[17] 'British'. This may refer to the 'Britannia' in Hoxton, north London, famous for its spectacular shows.

[18] An official appointed by debtors to ascertain what percentage may be paid out against outstanding debts.

special permit to take out any of my scenes as they were done. I didn't want to make unnecessary trouble for myself, so I never made a bother, but asked formally whenever I wanted a permit. The Receiver was a good enough fellow, and was very civil to me. We became quite friends. Schoolbred kept on working the show with the sanction of the liquidator. He had good assets, remember, and his engagements of star singers were fine.

'One day I came across him in a violent rage. When I asked him what had upset him he could hardly speak at first. At last when he got calmer he said:

'"It's enough to drive a man mad. Here I've been spending money like water to increase the taste for opera; and now, when I've a company that's simply gorgeous and things ought to hum along this Royal death[19] happens and knocks me right out. And the worst of it is it is all old debts except the landlord, and he's the worst of the bunch. Here have I been and restored this old rat's nest of his that had been so long empty that there's not a foot of timber in it that hasn't got the dry-rot. And now he goes and helps to make me a bankrupt – just as if that'll do him any good!"

'"But," I said, "surely that hasn't made you so violently angry this morning?"

'"Indirectly it has!"

'"How is that?" I asked.

'I have just got an offer from America – a magnificent offer – one that would make any manager get up and dance for joy. A fortune, sir, a fortune – a gigantic fortune. Every big town in the United States and Canada and Mexico and South America, where they're all crazy for opera, to follow."

'"But surely," I said, "that is a thing to be glad about, not angry. Why on earth should you stamp about with rage just because unexpectedly fortune has been put within your grasp?"

'"That is just the flaming aggravation of it all."

'"I'm afraid I don't understand," I said.

'"Oh, *you* don't understand, don't you?" he said, with a bitterness of sarcasm in his tones which showed that the wildness of

---

[19] If based on history, this might refer to the death of Prince Albert, Consort to Queen Victoria, in 1861, though his death was unlikely to have been treated so flippantly.

his rage had passed. "Then *I* had better explain to you. What is the use of putting fortune in my grasp – and then not letting me grasp it?"

'"It may be very silly of me, Mr Schoolbred," I said, "but still I don't understand."

'"How can I take the golden opportunity when I can't get away from here? Haven't we got bailiffs in the place! Isn't there an Official Receiver! How am I to get to America when these won't let a thing leave the Opera House? You can't play Grand Opera without scenery and properties and costumes, stupid! Here we are with sixteen operas – the best and most popular of them, all ready for the road – and yet we can't get even started. They are all rehearsed and perfect in every detail. I have every one of the artists on two years' engagements at English salary, but to play where and when I please. If I could get to America any time within the next two months there is nothing that could stand between me and success. There's no opposition whatever, and they couldn't get up one in the time. Moreover, I have all the popular artists – every one of them. Aye, and they would have to help me for a month at the beginning on half salaries or no salaries at all, and pay their own personals in addition. For they're in a cleft stick. They are engaged to me, so they can't play with anyone else; and if I don't play them they can't play at all. And yet here I am – here are we all – hung up for want of the sticks and rags.[20] It's cruel! It's wicked! It's vile! If I could only get away out of this."

'Whilst he was talking a thought had come to me that made me very uneasy. How would all this affect me? Since I had been allowed to take out some of my own work that was urgent, things had got worse. *Then* disaster had been only threatening; now it had come. How would it be if they were to seize my things as well as old Schoolbred's! Then it flashed across me how wise had been the provision of the lease, for now they couldn't take my goods. Old Schoolbred had been watching my face narrowly; now he said, suddenly:

'"But I can't get away. None of us can get away. They have formal possession of everything in the house – and they'll bally well

---

20 Scenery and costumes.

take care to hold very tight so that they can seize everything when the time comes."

'"They can't seize my things!" I said. He rubbed his hands in delight.

'"That is so; you have a lease. I am glad of that." He thought awhile, and his face fell. For a moment there was a gleam, but it faded as quickly as it had come, and there was on him a look of hopeless sadness. It was in his voice, too, when he spoke next:

'"That Receiver is a leery[21] fellow - a sly, cold-blooded, heartless villain! There won't be much consideration for either you or me in the long run. I say, Turner Smith, a word of caution in your ear: Don't you trust him, and if you can help it don't ask any favours from him. Later on it may be all right; but at present he has to think of himself."

'"How do you mean?" said I.

'"He has to hold down his own job. He may be willing enough to help you; but his first duty is to the Court that employs him."

'Two or three days afterwards he came up to my room and said he had a commission to give me, and explained that he was going to make a new departure in opera.

'I am going to show them a realistic up-to-date opera; in fact, an old-fashioned Adelphi[22] drama - except that it will be all sung. It is to be called *For the Love of an Actress*. The scenes will be all theatre interiors except the third act, which is to be the wicked Billionaire's palace in Park Lane.[23] The Soprano is, of course, the heroine, and is the daughter of the Scenic Artist. She loves with mutual affection the Tenor, who is the unacknowledged son of the Billionaire by a secret marriage. The Billionaire (Bass, of course), who is a widower, wants to marry her, but she refuses. Then he gets mad and carries her off. The Tenor breaks into the Park Lane palace, and there is a great trio, which is ended by the King[24] and all his nobles, who are

---

21 'leery': knowing.

22 The Adelphi Theatre in the Strand, London. It was famous for spectacular, often patriotic dramas, particularly in the 1890s.

23 Park Lane is in fashionable Mayfair in the West End of London and runs down the eastern side of Hyde Park.

24 In 1908 the British throne was occupied by King Edward VII.

coming to dine, arriving unexpectedly early. Of course, they are all in their robes as they are dining with a Billionaire. The King happens to have in his pocket the marriage certificate of the Billionaire's first wife, and also of the birth of her son. So then and there he holds a meeting of the House of Lords, and they find the Billionaire guilty. The Headsman is called in, and he is going to be executed when the Soprano in a passionate prayer appeals to the King to save him. 'Spare, oh spare, Most Gracious Ruler, the grandsire of my unborn child!' So the Billionaire makes over his money to his son, whom the King creates a Duke, and all ends happily. How does that strike you, my boy? Eh?"

'"Well, as you ask me," I said, "I think it the balliest rot I ever heard in my life!" He slapped me on the shoulder with quite a merry air, as he explained:

'"Right, my boy, right as rain. Rot is no name for it! That's why I'm so hopeful about it. We'll play it with grim seriousness, and there won't be a scene that isn't prickly with the most outrageous breaches of *convenance.*[25] All London will rush to see it and laugh their very souls out. The music is fine, full of melody – just the thing for empty-headed smart society that wants to be amused. We're going to be on the pig's back,[26] I can tell you, my boy." He then proceeded to make me a very handsome offer for painting the scenes. He said he had worked it out on a generous basis, because he wouldn't be able to pay me till the opera was out. That was reasonable enough, so I agreed. Then he told me that for the first act we couldn't do better than reproduce the painting room exactly as it stood. "It looks business, you know. All the appliances for scene painting ready with the painter at work – a fine bit of realism. That will fetch the public in itself. The Tenor will make up like you – Willie Larkom will arrange all that. And as it will be good to show the public what an expensive thing an opera is, you, or rather he, will have twelve assistants who will all be made up like the best known members of the Royal Academy. Of course, they are chorus, and will sing a song with a queer catch in the refrain – a

---

25 Conventional propriety.

26 This means a double win. Riding 'piggy-back' implies conveyance upon the source of a full meal, as well as the food itself.

discord like the creaking of a windlass."[27] At the door he turned and said:

'"By the way - two things: not a word of this to a soul. The surprise will be half the battle, and I want to get it out quick, so you must get the first act done as soon as ever you can. As this is to be a reproduction of your own *atelier*, and the painting is in your own hands, there is no need for a model. You can start at once. In order to save time, I have had the flats primed and ready - full stage, my boy, and new canvas framed in folding panels for travelling - and not a wrinkle in the lot. And please note, I want that scene - it is where the lovers meet - to be brilliant moonlight. You must have a practical moon - a big one - shining in through the glass roof. I want to show a new moonlight[28] effect."

'I slipped into my work, and three days afterwards I was almost ready. I kept my doors locked, and not a soul was in the secret except old Schoolbred and myself, and, of course, my own people; but I could trust them.

'It was too bad that I had a delay; but I suppose it could not be helped. It turned out that Wilbur Winston had fixed the date for *Manfred*, and wanted to get in the Thunderstorm Scene[29] at once, so that he could start the lighting rehearsals. He had decided four days before, but had not announced it, except to a few friends, till he was ready to take rehearsals in hand. I arranged with him that the stuff should be brought into the British on the following Saturday night after the play was over. I got the police permit, which was necessary, for there was a devil of a lot of stuff and huge stuff too. Some of the built pieces were over forty feet long. There was one panorama cloth, which was to go round nearly the whole of the three sides of the stage. This would have to travel on two timber carts roped together head and tail. I was to come early on Sunday and see to its being put together on the British stage, and Winston would begin the lighting with a full staff that night. Rehearsals were

---

27 A machine used for hoisting and hauling. In this case, for raising and lowering the scene 'frame'.

28 This word is used in an ambiguous sense, as will become apparent.

29 This refers to the second scene in the verse-play by Byron, in the mountains of the Jungfrau. The melancholy Count Manfred seeks death by suicide on the cliff edge, but is 'saved' by the arrival of a chamois hunter.

to follow from Monday.

'Old Schoolbred was most helpful in arranging things. He certainly could hustle when he put his back into it! He undertook to arrange and look after the carting. I told him how many carts I should require, and the kind. He had a carting contract with the London Haulage Company based on men and horses and hours, so I knew he couldn't best me about the price. It was necessary to keep an eye on the old man, for he was the shiftiest old rascal I ever came across. I told my assistant to look after him, and he undertook to see the stuff safely out. I had, of course, arranged with the Receiver that the scenery should be allowed to come out. He was very nice about it, and I had his written permit in due form. He had not been a bit like what old Schoolbred said of him. I know now even better how false the old trickster was.

'Schoolbred had asked me to set the new scene on the stage – well up,[30] so that it should not be in the way of rehearsals on Saturday after the day-men had gone home. We did not play on that night, so it was easy to arrange. I got my own men and a few that the Governor sent in; the regular day-men of the Opera House were away for the afternoon. The Governor had fixed the day for the "outing" of the theatre staff and employees, and they were having a big dinner up in Islington.[31] The old man provided dinner for them "very handsomely," as they said. It was conventional lighting – plain gas, and all overhead, just as we used in the painting room. Old Schoolbred came and saw it set himself. We didn't want any fuss, so there was no one there except those actually at work. He was very complimentary about my work. He said he couldn't have believed that anyone could have made the dull old painting room so luxurious. "If I had thought you could have done that with it I'm blessed if I would have rented it to you at the money!" he said, in a burst of candour unusual to him.

'"But you asked me to specially," I answered. "Don't you

---

[30] Stages were always 'raked' at this time – that is, sloped to offer full views to the audience wherever they are seated. 'Up' is furthermost from the stage, so therefore refers to the back of the stage. 'Downstage' is by the footlights and orchestra. Nowadays many stages are flat.

[31] Islington is an area of north central London, and has always been a popular theatre area.

remember you said that you wanted it to look like a miracle of artistic luxury. I took some pains, I can tell you, to paint in all that fine old furniture. Dagmar let me take some drawings in his place; he said he'd be blessed if he'd let his things come here –"

'"Oh, I ain't complaining," he answered. "In fact, I intended to furnish the place up a bit myself, so as I thought I would have some practical safes and things I went to his place and got them – paid him for them too; he wouldn't let them come without. When he told me in confidence which pieces you had taken as models, I purchased them. They are in my own room at the present moment. I'll send them down here to-morrow, so as to be ready for rehearsals."

'There was only one disagreeable incident that day, and strangely enough it came from an unexpected quarter. The men in possession got shirty[32] because they had not been asked to the beano.[33] It was an outrageous position for them to take, when their only duty was to be on and not off the premises. But men in their position can give a lot of trouble by simply doing nothing; and everyone who has had the misfortune of having them in the house knows that it is well to keep them in good humour. I was a bit anxious myself, for, after all, they were the servants of the Court, and they might ruin me by wilfully making some mistake about my permit, and I couldn't get it put right till Monday. If Winston didn't get his Thunderstorm Scene on the Saturday night he might get shirty in his turn and repudiate the whole transaction – then where should I be?'

'In the soup,[34] my boy; in the soup!' said the Low Comedian.

'H-s-s-h!' said the Company in chorus; they wanted to hear what happened.

'However, Schoolbred soothed them with the promise of a dinner for themselves. On the Saturday night I saw the men in possession just sitting down to dinner. The old man had certainly done them well. He had a dinner sent in for them from the Old

[32] From having one's shirt pulled out and freed (unbuttoned for ease) in a fight. Hence, in a bad temper or annoyed.

[33] 'beano': bean-feast. Employer's dinner for the workers.

[34] A well-known 'cannibal' joke. To be in big trouble.

Red Post Restaurant – soup and fish, and an entrée, and joints and sweets and savoury and cheese and dessert and coffee. Moreover, there was champagne up to the masthead, and liqueurs, and brandy and whisky and cigars after. It was all laid out at once, and they looked as if they were enjoying the very sight. Said I to myself: "There won't be any trouble with these fellows about my permit. This banquet of Heliogabalus[35] will make them blind. Moreover, they will be blind in another form before very long. It'll take them till to-morrow afternoon to sleep *this* off!"

'My assistant, Rooke, was there to see our work off, so I went home to have a good sleep. I knew there would be no time for sleep or rest when Winston began to rehearse his great scene.

'On Sunday, just as I had got my scene set up in the British ready for Winston to see it Rooke came in looking very excited, and took me on one side:

'"Oh, that infernal scoundrel!" he began. He was so excited that I found it difficult to get him to begin. However, he started at last:

'"That old scoundrel Schoolbred! What do you think that he did! It turns out that he made a contract for America – the one he told you was offered him – undertaking to stage sixteen full operas. He had them all ready, as you know; but his trouble was to get them off, for they were in the hands of the Court, with men in possession to watch them. Well, he evidently fixed last night to get off. He had a big Atlantic steamer, the *Rockefeller*,[36] ready in the docks, and put the whole company, staff and chorus and all, aboard last evening. Then at midnight he had a train of carts ready – there must have been a hundred of them – and on the head of getting out our one scene he carted off the whole lot out of the Opera House. They didn't begin that work, of course, till after our job, for I was there and might have been dangerous. Of course, I left when our own stuff went. In fact, I came on the last cart, and saw it all brought into the British. That yarn about the new opera was all bunkum. The new scene, too, was only a blind to keep our lot quiet and

[35] A Roman Emperor famous for his debauchery.

[36] The ship is named in honour of the US philanthropist John Davison Rockefeller (1839-1937).

disarm suspicion. The moon was his joke. He had the sofas put in as he said he would, and had the bailiffs carried in and laid on them. They may be there yet for all I know. It would take a whole day to make *them* conscious. But the job seemed to the police and others continuous – they had the order of the Receiver and the police permit, and there was nothing seemingly out of order. When once the carts got off it was no one's business to enquire where they were going to. So that is how the old rascal shot the moon.[37] He is off on blue water by this time with his whole outfit, and will come back with a fortune. The landlord won't grumble, because Schoolbred must pay his rent, or else they will attach him for stealing their scenery. Nor will the Receiver either, for he is in for a fat job for at least a year to come, nothing to do, and sure of being paid. Even the men in possession whom he diddled will have to be kept here, and they will have an easy time. I daresay they will expect to have every day a blow-out such as they had last night. But they won't get it. They don't know Schoolbred. He is all very generous when he wants anything, but he don't give something for nothing."

'But he did – for once. Before he came back from America he sent me the receipt from the Receiver of my rent for the whole time. He had paid it himself.'

Just then there was a distant noise which came drifting down on the wind. All started to their feet. There was the shrill sound of a whistle. Presently there was a loud knock at the side door of the saloon, and the door was dragged open, to the accompaniment of drifting snow and piercingly cold wind. Two railway men came in, shutting with difficulty the door behind them. One of them shouted out:

'It's a' richt! A snow-ploo wi' twa engines[38] has been sent on frae Dundee.[39] A rotary that has bored a road through the drifts.

---

[37] To do a 'Moonlight Flit' means to move out without paying one's debts. A traditional piece of roguery with tour theatricals in bad lodgings which is why landladies demanded their money on Friday nights.

[38] 'It is all right. A snow plough with two engines.'

[39] 'frae': from Dundee. Scottish city on the north side of the Firth of Tay, scene of the Tay Bridge disaster of 1879, which means the train would now cross on the new rail bridge.

We're firin' up fast, and ye'll a' sleep in yer beds the nicht[40] - somewhere. An' A'm thinkin' we could dae wi' some o' yer Johnny Walker[41] - hot.'

THE END

---

[40] 'nicht': night.

[41] 'dae wi': do with some of your Johnny Walker, the Scottish whisky distillers still going strong.